FOXWEPT ARRAY

BOOK 3

BEAUTY, UNMASKED

A FUTURISTIC ROMANCE RETELLING OF BEAUTY AND THE BEAST

A.W. CROSS

GLORY BOX PRESS

Beauty, Unmasked

Published by Glory Box Press
British Columbia, Canada.
gloryboxpress@gmail.com

First edition, 2019

ISBN 978-1-9995711-7-7

Cover design by Danielle Fine
Interior design and formatting by Glory Box Press
Editing by Danielle Fine

FOR H,
MY BEAUTIFUL BEAST.

BEAUTY, UNMASKED

ONE

It was Beauty's father who delivered her to the Beast.

He wasn't really her father—not by blood, anyway—but Raphael Quinn insisted that all the waifs under his protection call him so, and Beauty was more than happy to oblige. If it hadn't been for him, she may have ended up with another master, or, worse, dead. The war still took many victims inside The Vault—you didn't need to be staring the enemy in the eye for them to kill you.

No, she had gotten lucky.

At least he cares if we have enough to eat and an education. Otherwise, we'd be as ignorant as the Nightforge. She closed her book carefully, slipping a small silver chain between the pages to hold her place. *And we wouldn't have so many books.*

The other scavengers didn't care about books, but Raphael valued them almost as much as he did the rare antiquities and oddities that were their bread and butter. "There's nothing more valuable than knowledge," he would often remind them.

He ducked through the doorway now, a deceptive man, tall with an oddly youthful face and a slow, languid voice. His competitors often underestimated him, much to their detriment. He was like a golem, soft clay on the outside, but a killer underneath.

"Would you two mind doing that somewhere else?" He frowned pointedly at two of Beauty's "siblings." Violet and Arjun had been making eyes at each other across the scarred wooden table all morning, Arjun's foot repeatedly confusing Beauty's legs with that of his "princess," as he called Violet. "Preferably *after* your work is done for the day."

Chastened, the couple gathered their dirty dishes and scuttled off to the kitchen.

In less than an hour, I'll be stumbling over them in some dark alleyway as they paw at each other.

Beauty didn't get it. Arjun was good-looking enough, but their work was so important. And until recently, both he and Violet had been so zealously committed to the cause that Beauty had had to turn away from them often, her odd moments of doubt a disgrace. Now, their obligations seemed secondary, but how could anything be more important? If they didn't do their duty, they would all die—overrun by the intruders that had already destroyed most of their world.

Time had blurred the details of the invasion for Beauty. She was only a child when the war began, and her memories of her parents' faces—her *real* mother and father—had eroded with time. They had died early on, ordinary civilians unprepared for the onslaught that would decimate the already sparsely populated region until, finally, Wakelight became The Vault, named for the domed force field that now covered the city. It had saved them, continued to protect them, and it was their responsibility to ensure it would do so until the war was over. Until then, it kept the nightmare at bay, the only clue the far-off sounds of gunfire and falling bombs, the scent of scorched earth.

"What are you reading, Beauty?" Father took a seat across the table from her. "Anything interesting? It must be, for you to look so tired."

Beauty ducked her head as warmth crept into her cheeks. She normally wouldn't have left her room with that particular book in her hand, but she'd been so caught up in it, so transported by the magic between its pages, that she'd been unable to put it down. Sitting at the tables, ignored by the others, she'd lost track of time. Again.

"It's nothing, just—" She rose hurriedly from the table. "Just something I picked up." She backed away and was almost clear when Father seized her wrist. "Beauty?"

She understood his concern. Some of the books they recovered held subjects considered inflammatory or forbidden—treatises against war, against violence. Tomes that encouraged the reader to lay down their arms and avoid conflict. The kind that would weaken patriotism and undermine the war effort. *Those* Father made sure to destroy right away. But this book wasn't one of those—it was far, far worse.

He stared at the cover, his eyebrows drawing together in disbelief. "A *romance* novel?" He glanced up at her, the beginning of a smile curling the corner of his mouth.

The flush turned into a blazing inferno. What would he think of her now? It was the sort of frivolous thing he expected of Violet, not her. She was the serious one, the only one of his children who truly loved her job tracking down and recovering rarities. She'd spend hours digging in the corner of an abandoned building on nothing more than a

3

hunch or a feeling, though her efforts were more often rewarded than not. It was her dedication that had made him so fond of her. Well, that would all change now, wouldn't it? Now that he knew what a fool she really was.

She didn't understand it herself, her fascination with these books. On the surface, the subject matter seemed ridiculous and trivial—two people finding true love amidst adversary. Nothing in the world could've been less important right now. Love could wait until peace came. Everyone knew that. And yet...considering how many of the novels they'd retrieved over the years, there must've a been a time when matters of the heart were of the utmost importance, when there was nothing more people could've wanted from life than to find their soulmate. The books, their notions of one true love were nonsense—her mortification proved that—but she just couldn't seem to stay away from them. Just like she couldn't ignore Violet and Arjun when they touched or whispered intimately to each other. She was torn between contempt for their silliness and longing for someone to look at her the way they did each other.

"I'm surprised." Father considered her, his expression faintly bemused. "But you are eighteen now, so I guess I shouldn't be."

It just kept getting worse. Beauty squirmed, desperate to snatch the book from his hands, dive back into her bed, pull the covers over her head, and wait for the world to disappear. Could someone die of embarrassment?

"I...I just— I'm sorry."

His expression softened as he smiled at her. "Sorry? Why would you be sorry?"

"I know it's stupid. I know I should be reading something..."

"More important?"

"Yes."

"Beauty, nothing is more important than love."

"What?" It was the last thing she'd ever expected him to say. Laugh, yes. Be angry? Maybe. But the way he was looking at her now was kind, almost wistful. Maybe, even after all these years, she didn't really know him at all.

"It's true. But it's a luxury few remember now, and even fewer can afford." He smiled, gazing past her into another time. "Once, love was responsible for the rise and fall of many a society. Wars were fought over it, music and art revolved around it..." He shook himself and returned to the present. He glanced at Beauty and his gaze hardened. "But those days have passed. Never forget that. People who do, like your brother and sister, can destroy themselves and those around them with it. Love is a poisoned chalice now, Beauty, so be aware of its taint."

Beauty hung her head. "I'll put the book back now. I promise I won't read them again."

Father pressed two fingers under her chin and raised her face to look at him. "That's not what I'm saying, Beauty, not at all. I think you should keep reading these books."

"You do?"

"Yes. Find refuge in them, let them be the romance in your life. It's the only way these days. Go out, do your work, then when you come home, they'll be here waiting for you. No danger, no risk of betrayal, no obligation." He tapped the cover of the book. "This love is the only safe kind of love. In fact," he rose and handed her the book then rolled his shoulders, "when I get home, I know a few you might be interested in."

Beauty stared after him as he strode away. Who would've thought the old scrapper was so sentimental? Still, *him* knowing was one thing, but she'd die if any of the others found out about her guilty pleasure, even Red, and *she* was Beauty's best friend. Across the room, Father opened the assignment book, the cord hanging from the old copper bell next to him brushing his arm.

It would be only a few minutes before the bell pealed through the burrow, so Beauty dashed back to her room at the far end of the warren. All the Guilds lived underground, seeking refuge in case The Vault was ever breached. The complex stone network had been built long before Wakelight, unused and ignored until nearly a decade ago, when the first rumbles of war began. The old maze under the city had been cleared as a precaution—one that paid off when the city was destroyed. Now they huddled underground like rodents, scrambling to the surface during the day to hunt. It had taken Beauty weeks to get used to living underground, but now she enjoyed the coziness of their close quarters.

Red, who was also Beauty's roommate, was turning the air blue as she searched under her bed. Beauty took advantage of her distraction and slipped the book under her pillow. Breathing a sigh of relief, she joined the other girl on the floor.

"What are you looking for?" She stuck her own head under the cot, but all she could see was dust and shadows.

Red flipped her auburn braid over her shoulder. "My stupid knife. I've lost it *again*."

Beauty pressed her lips together. Red's carelessness was a bone of contention between her and Father. Unless she found it, it would be the third one she'd lost this month. And she couldn't go out without it; it just wasn't safe. Competition was fierce and being shanked for something as ordinary as scrap metal wasn't unusual. With the higher-end goods the Hallow Hands were known for, a weapon—and the skill to use it—was a necessity. She raised her fingers to the just-healed ridge on her cheek—a gift from one of the Sightless Fall. "When did you see it last?"

"Yesterday. It's definitely here somewhere. I'm positive I put in in my box when I got home last night." She held out the empty case to Beauty. "I'm not going crazy, right? It's definitely not there."

Beauty shook her head. "Sorry, Red. It's definitely gone."

Red threw herself back onto her bed, her groan drowned out by the bell. They had only a few more seconds to get down to the kitchen. "He's going to kill me."

"Looking for this?" Leaning in the doorway was a tall, blond girl, a wicked blade dangling from her fingers.

"Thief! That's *my* knife." Red squared her shoulders and glared up at the older girl.

"Oh, quit your crying. I brought it back, didn't I?" She curled her lip. "Here, catch."

The knife turned end over end as it tore through the air toward Red, who reflexively reached out to try to catch it. It sliced into her palm as she fumbled. "Damn it, Kaitlin!" But the other girl was gone, her laughter floating back down the hallway.

"Are you okay?" Beauty grabbed her hand and turned it over. The cut was shallow, but infections

7

were more likely than not. "We'll have to put something on this before we go out."

"We're going to be late, though." Red glanced at the doorway and bounced on the balls of her feet.

"Better late than have you die or lose your arm."

"Thanks, Beauty. That makes me feel *so* much better."

Beauty rifled through her own box, a small, burnished wooden thing that held all her meager possessions. After finding some bandages that looked clean, she poured homemade disinfectant over the wound, biting her lip as the other girl hissed in pain. When it was as clean as she could make it, she wrapped Red's hand, pinching the edges of the cut together as tightly as she could.

"I just don't get what's wrong with Kaitlin." Red winced as Beauty tugged on the binding. "We're supposed to be on the same team."

"I know. You'd think she'd have better things to worry about." They all did. The Vault could only protect them from the horrors outside if they continued to fund it. "Like survival." She checked the bandage one last time. "That should do it. Come on, let's go before we get in trouble."

"Not that *you'll* get in trouble," the other girl grumbled as they sprinted down the hallway. "You're his favorite."

The others often teased Beauty about this, their joking voices belying the animosity in their eyes. She tried to downplay it as much as possible lest she find something sharp-toothed and hungry under her pillow. Father forbade outright aggression between his wards, but he viewed *some* competition as healthy. Still, despite the risks, there were certain advantages to being the favorite—the best sites, for example—even if she couldn't imagine why Father would prefer her. Beauty wasn't as fast as Red or strong as Felix. She didn't have Jere's charm or Kaitlin's ruthlessness. As part of a team she was awkward, unlike the well-oiled duo of Violet and Arjun. The only thing she actually had going for her was her true interest in the items they recovered. Perhaps that was enough.

"Well, maybe if you kept a better eye on your things—"

The tension in the room pulled Beauty up short. What was going on? Nothing looked different. Felix slouched against the wall like he always did, looking bored. Jere picked dirt from under his fingernails with the tip of his knife. Violet and Arjun stood close together, surreptitiously trying to hold hands without anyone noticing, and Kaitlin had her gaze locked on Father.

Business as usual, then.

But not for Father. Normally, when the Guild arrived to be handed their morning's assignments, he was waiting for them, arms crossed over his chest. They would begin with their heads bowed, whispering the Hallow Hands motto over and over in a swelling crescendo: *"Dedication, duty, defiance."*

Today, however, he paced at the head of the room. His face was pale with gray shadows under his eyes. Had he looked like that earlier? Beauty had been so distracted by her own embarrassment that she hadn't noticed. Whatever he had on his mind, it must be big. Father was unflappable—he'd had to be to rise to the position he was in now. One didn't become the head of a Vault Guild unless they had nerves of steel.

He raised an eyebrow as Beauty and Red skidded into the room but didn't chastise them. Also unusual. Father ran a very tight ship, and sloppiness wasn't often tolerated. Was his distraction to do with today's assignments? If so, she'd find out soon enough.

Father cleared his throat. "Right. Now that we're all here—" He directed his gaze at Beauty and Red, and Beauty's tension eased a bit. *There he is.* "We've got a big day ahead of us, so let's just get through this. Any questions, save for the end."

He flipped open his map book and gestured for the others to do the same. "Okay, Violet and Felix—"

"Wait." Violet held up a hand. "Why am I not with Arjun? We always work together."

Father narrowed his eyes. "Do I need to remind you what happened the last time a couple continued working together?"

Rachel and Galan. Their loss still sat heavily in her chest. But Father was right. When you began putting someone else's safety before your own, you made mistakes based on emotion. Fatal mistakes.

Violet hung her head as Arjun swallowed hard. "Father, we won't—" His mouth snapped shut as Father raised a hand.

"You're right. You won't. What you will do is take your assignment and carry it out. Or you can stay away from each other."

Arjun's eyes flashed. "You can't—"

"*Or* you can find yourself a new Guild." Father didn't blink, though the muscle in his jaw flexed.

It was a serious threat. Trying to find a new Guild at Arjun's age would be difficult. And to have to start at the bottom... Not all the Guild leaders were as honorable as Father. He might come off as a hardass to the rest of The Vault, but behind the closed door of the warren, his charges were safe. From him, and from each other.

Arjun stared at Father a moment longer, his chin up. The rest of the Guild held their breaths as the seconds ticked by. *Please, just look down.*

As though he'd heard her, Arjun dropped his gaze to the floor and stepped away from Violet. The pain in her eyes made Beauty's stomach knot, but Father was right. Love was a risk they couldn't afford. She ached to reach out and squeeze Violet's hand, but the other girl would never forgive her. Weakness wasn't something that should be public, even here.

"As I was saying, Violet and Felix, you'll be heading to the southeast sector. I've had a tip-off about some old art there, although no details. Just bring back whatever you can get your hands on."

Felix shrugged in acknowledgment and pushed himself off the wall. Violet glared at him, her mouth a thin line.

"Jere, you'll be going with Arjun and Kaitlin to the southern sector. It's a bit of a mess there right now, but some of the ruins shifted and opened up a cache yesterday. The other Guilds haven't discovered it yet, so get in there and secure it." He raised an eyebrow at them. "I don't have to tell you to be careful—but keep an extra eye out. I'm sure I'm not the only one who knows about this."

Violet blanched. Fighting wasn't Arjun's strong suit, and Father knew it. Was he trying to teach her a lesson? Of all the items the Guilds scavenged for the war effort, the artifacts from the past were the most highly prized. The Vault was located deep in Heartcrown, one of the first regions of the Blackmoth Republic to have been settled, the old stone metropolis of Beauty's beloved home built over even older settlements. No other part of the Republic had such rich history, and now it was being sold off or traded piece by piece to supply the energy shield of The Vault. Artifacts were worth a huge number of points to the Guilds, and not a few had been killed over the years in claiming it. Beauty only hoped that they could win the war before their history was lost for good.

Before the war, before The Vault, the city had been run by an artificial intelligence. Named after the municipality it oversaw, the Wakelight AI had used a steady stream of information collected from sensors all over the city to manage its resources and assets. Every citizen also had a chip implanted in the back of their neck that gathered data and allowed the system to make their decisions for them.

But a few years after the war began, Wakelight had fallen silent. The only sign it still existed was the shell of The Vault itself. Everything else had ceased to run—including communication with the outside world. Now days were spent doing two things—trying desperately to keep themselves alive and giving every single thing they could grow or scavenge or build to the war effort.

Future for the Faithful. Beauty said it to herself every morning when she woke, and every night as she closed her eyes. One day, they would all be free.

Kaitlin grinned at the sallowness of Arjun's expression. She seemed to have a death wish, attacking the more dangerous assignments with a bewildering relish. But why? What did she have to die for? It wasn't like she'd lost any more than the rest of them.

"And finally, Red and Beauty, you'll be heading back to the literary quarter. I want you to go over that depository one more time. I can't help but think we've missed something."

It was all Beauty could do not to clap. She tried to keep her expression neutral as the others turned their eyes toward her.

Kaitlin scoffed. "A book run. Shocking."

Book runs were notoriously easy. Requests were pretty slim, but every so often, they would get a call for books to give to the soldiers, to ease their suffering and give them an escape. Although the others cared nothing for books, retrieving them was simple—*and* the other Guilds rarely bothered with them. Get in, get out.

Beauty didn't care much about that. She loved the books. She never knew what incredible adventure she was going to dig out of the ruins. Father would let her keep some of them, a secret from the others. And Beauty liked to think of those that were shipped out in the hands of the men and women fighting tirelessly for her survival. Often, she scrawled a note in her unpracticed hand—an expression of thanks or support. It was silly, but it helped ease her conscience that she was safe in The Vault, while every day the soldiers woke up to what might be their last sunrise. Her fingers tingled with anticipation. Today felt like a good day.

"Do you have a problem, Kaitlin?" Father glared at her, his expression hard.

"Me? Oh no, Father. *Never.*"

He looked at her for a moment longer then cleared his throat. "I'll be taking a shipment to the

13

Beast today." His voice was steady, but Beauty knew him well enough to sense the current underneath it. *He's scared.*

Before today, she wouldn't have thought it possible. But then, Father had a very good reason to be afraid. *Everyone* was frightened of the Beast, their sector's liaison with the outside world. Everyone except Stiles, the mountain of a man who usually delivered their shipments. *He* never seemed to be afraid of the monster they only whispered about.

The Beast was rumored to be more machine than human, a merciless creature literally without a heart. His face was cold steel, the countenance of a demon with curling horns and teeth filed to points. He was thought to live deep in the bowels of the earth, the miles of rock above his head the only thing strong enough to contain his rage. Of those who went to seek him with one complaint or another, none returned. If you were bringing him a shipment, you had a much better chance of survival—but it wasn't guaranteed. Foreboding grew in Beauty, a wild thing curling around her ribcage.

"What happened to Stiles?" Felix was no longer nonchalant. He stood with his arms crossed over his chest, shifting his weight from one foot to the other.

Father sighed and shook his head. "I'm not entirely sure. It was some kind of accident—"

"Did the Beast kill him?"

"I don't know, Beauty." His mouth was grim. "But it's a possibility." His tone suggested it was a certainty.

"Are you sure you should be going then? Can't you get someone else to do it? Even at a higher cost?"

Felix's wariness was understandable. What if Father went to the Beast and didn't return? What would happen to the rest of them? How long would they be able to cover Father's disappearance before the other Guilds moved on their turf? The alliances and territories they held now were shaky at best.

"I'll be fine." But his taut face looked anything but.

"You—"

"I *said* I'll be fine." Father's face darkened and the vein in his neck throbbed as the others stared at him, mouths agape.

He's not scared, he's terrified.

And suddenly, so was she. Perhaps they should go with him. Then they could—

"Don't even think about following me, any of you. If I wanted company, I would've asked. The Beast has made it very clear that he'll see me and me alone." He shot Kaitlin a warning glance. "I mean it. All you'll be doing is putting us both in even more danger."

The silence that followed was as unusual as his fear. It was broken only by the scuff of Felix's boots on the concrete floor.

"Well, what are you all waiting for? Get going. I'll see you tonight, I promise." He pointed toward the door. "*Go.*"

Beauty turned with the others and made her way out of the warren, Arjun seething at her side. All the joy at searching for lost books was gone. This was no longer a good day. But it would be a day she would always remember.

TWO

Cillian found himself in the library. Of course, it wasn't really a library, just a room filled with books, but thinking of it in more civilized terms always helped. He told Cybel that sorting and shelving them was simply a more efficient way to pick and choose them when the time came, but whenever he was troubled, he found himself here, running his fingers over the spines. Paper books had been a rarity even before the war, and now... His gut clenched. So much had been lost.

Fine thoughts for a soldier.

But he wasn't a soldier anymore. Now he was a monster. He couldn't even really feel the spines beneath his left hand, only the odd sensation of a texture different than the smooth metal of his own fingers. That would change one day, of course, when his duty was done. But for now, he would have to be content with nostalgia.

He glanced at the tomes his hand hovered over then snatched it back with a bitter laugh. Romance novels. Ridiculous things. Why he bothered keeping them, he had no idea. They were almost offensive, the perfect-bodied men and women with no concern in life but whether the other person shared what seemed to him a dangerous infatuation. Had people ever really lived like that? He certainly hadn't. Not before the war, not during, and certainly not after. How could someone be so wrapped up in another person that they would die for them? He shook his head. Such sentiments didn't exist now.

And I'm glad for that.

No, you're not. You're just bitter because no one will ever love you that way.

He bit the inside of his cheek. *That* kind of thinking did nothing to improve his temper. Where the hell was Raphael Quinn? The man should've delivered his shipment hours ago. It was bad enough that Stiles was dead...but Quinn? Cillian didn't know enough about the man. If he thought Cillian could be kept waiting...well, that was why they called him the Beast.

The Beast.

He'd been called by the nickname for so long, even he'd begun to think of himself like that.

Who are you trying to kid? It's because you are a beast. A monster. They'd call you much worse if they knew the truth.

Enough. He stalked from the library, his mind made up. If Quinn wasn't going to come to Cillian, Cillian would have to go to him.

This requisition, though frivolous, came from someone very important. The Beast stopped by the control room one last time as he slipped leather gloves over his hands. He *should've* kept them uncovered, all the better to maintain his reputation, but if these people found out what he really was... The stories they told helped keep his fearsome reputation, but only because nobody truly believed them.

Just as he turned away from his surveillance screens, movement on one of them caught his eye.

A man staggered down the corridor, cradling one arm in the other. His face was bloodied on one side, and dark footprints trailed after him.

Cillian swore. It was Quinn. But he didn't seem to be carrying a damn thing with him.

A few minutes later, Quinn tumbled to his knees on the threshold. Cillian hauled him the rest of the way through by the collar of his jacket then stepped out into the passage and listened intently. Nothing. He closed the door and slid the locks shut, one after the other. When he turned around, Quin was sprawled out on the floor, facedown.

Irritation bit at Cillian. What the hell had happened? Quinn reeked of Demon's Breath, the liquid that passed for alcohol in The Vault. But surely the man wasn't foolish enough to get drunk while carrying out orders? Well, Cillian would get to the bottom of it, and god help the man if he didn't have a damn good excuse. The people Cillian worked for were not patient, nor were they merciful, and it would be his neck on the line if they didn't get what they'd asked for.

He dragged Quinn to a ratty old sofa in a back room and hoisted him up onto it, the drunk man's head tilting over the back. A bucket of cold, dirty water was next.

I really should just slap him out of it.

But breaking his face wasn't going to get Cillian what he needed. Experience had taught him that.

As soon as the first splash of water touched Quinn's face, his eyes and mouth shot open and he choked on the filthy liquid. Gagging, he raised his hands over his head until the bucket had finished its onslaught.

"Hey, a—" But as the water cleared from his eyes, he seemed to realize where he was and who he was talking to. The color drained from his face and he gagged again, though his mouth was now dry.

He'd better not throw up. Or worse.

He wouldn't be the first one, but Cillian was in no mood to clean up after incontinent scavengers. Not today. He crossed his arms over his chest and took a step back. "Raphael Quinn."

Quinn peered up at him from under his soaked forelock, water dripping from his chin. His chest rose and fell swiftly.

"Where is the requisition?"

"I don't have it, but I—"

Cillian leaned toward him. "Why not?"

Quinn shrank back. "I was attacked." He brushed his fingers over a large graze on his forehead.

"And?"

"And they took it."

Cillian stared at Quinn, waiting.

The other man held out for only a few seconds. "It wasn't my fault. I—"

"It wasn't your fault? You stink of liquor."

"I know, but—"

"But what? Your country asks you to acquire something extremely valuable, and rather than bring it straight here as you were commissioned to do, you decide to go drinking instead?"

"No! Yes. I—" He clamped his jaw shut under Cillian's glare.

Cillian swore inwardly. Quinn wasn't the first man to need liquid courage to make a delivery. His reputation was a double-edged sword. On one hand, it made it much easier to keep up the charade of The

Vault, but on the other, it caused normally brave and honorable men to degrade themselves in fear. The initial thrill of his power had long since gone.

If only they knew how little power I actually have.

Quinn was still jabbering away. "But I can make it up to you."

"You have more First jewelry?"

"No. But I can get you something else, something double the value. My team—"

"I need First jewelry."

"Well, you're going to get it. Just not from me."

Cillian sighed. "How?"

"I'm pretty sure I know who rolled me. I'd bet the shirt off my back she'll be knocking on your door before tomorrow with an item you just *might* be interested in—for double our price, of course." His voice was bitter.

He was right. That was usually how it worked. As the city was picked over and many resources became scarcer, the Guilds had begun to use more than their deductive talents to find the most valuable merchandise. It wasn't just the compensation they received—a pittance. Rather, it was the prestige, allotted in points, that the Guilds chased. The promise that when the war was over, those points would be tallied and parlayed into the Guild's standing and circumstance in the new world. A beautiful lie.

"That may be so, but that doesn't absolve you."

"I know, but as I said, I'll make it up to you. My Guild is one of the best there is, B— Sir."

Beast. There it was. Anger rose before he swiftly tamped it down. It was his own doing that

20

they saw him this way. It had been a necessity. But that didn't make it any less infuriating.

"One of the best? That's a pretty bold claim considering you're sitting here empty-handed and covered in sewer water."

"We are! Do you remember that rose prism you received a few months back? Well, that was us. Our Beauty found it. She has an uncanny ability to locate the rarest items. She reads a lot, you see, including maps and—"

Cillian did remember the prism. It had been a tricky find, no doubt. But other than bragging, what did that have to do with anything? "I don't—"

"She found the prism? That *is* impressive." The voice came from behind Cillian, and he winced. The last thing he needed right now was Cybel getting involved. The little bot was too social for its own good, a defect in its programming.

He turned and spoke through gritted teeth. "Yes. It is. But it doesn't have anything to—"

"We could use some more help around here." She ignored the tone of his voice, like always. The small humanoid robot was a source of both great affection and great annoyance. "Weren't you saying that just the other day? And if she's as good as he claims..."

While it was true that he and Cybel could use more help, there was no way in hell he was going to take on some brainwashed Guild member, or anyone else from The Vault, for that matter. And Cybel bloody well knew it. It was too risky. Besides, why would he want to deal with people any more than he already did? He kept his interactions to a minimum—it was better for everyone that way.

Out of the question, no matter how good she might be.

21

The color leached from Quinn's face. "No! I wasn't suggesting— No. Absolutely not."

His refusal rankled. *I'm too used to getting what I want.* But more than that, the Guilds had sworn unyielding loyalty to The Vault's cause, to give whatever, whenever they could to continue the war effort. Some, like the Nightforge, took it to extremes, their members little more than skin and bones as they donated everything beyond what they needed for bare survival. *Glory Through Sacrifice.* Quinn had no right to refuse, and Cillian couldn't let him. If word somehow got out that someone had refused his order... The smallest of rebellions could lead to larger ones, ones he couldn't control.

There were rules the Guilds were expected to abide by: keep to their assigned sectors, do not interfere with other Guilds, locate whatever items were required, give any items found to the cause, and never question orders. The Guilds, of course, flaunted some of these rules and Cillian knew it— the proof sat on the couch in front of him. Minor infractions he didn't have the time or the patience to deal with. But unquestioning loyalty? *That* was non-negotiable.

Besides, taking her would also serve as a warning to Quinn on a personal level. This Beauty, whoever she was, obviously meant a great deal to him, that he would refuse the Beast. A perverse spitefulness came over Cillian. He would teach Quinn a lesson, if only for a brief time. He would keep the girl for a week or two then send her back.

Cillian flexed his hands inside his gloves, making sure Quinn got the hint.

The horrified look on the man's face suggested he did.

"You would refuse me? And The Vault?"

Quinn faltered. "No. I— I just...I can't grant you that. Anything else. I have other Guild members who are even better than Beauty. You can have your pick of them. Plus, I'll get you goods of greater value—"

"No. I want her. This Beauty."

"But—" Quinn's chest hitched, as though he was going to vomit. Did she really mean that much to him?

"Unless you want to come in her place? It *was* your...mistake, after all."

Quinn stared at him as though it were a battle of wills. Yet only seconds later he broke, nodding like a senti doll. "Of course, of course. She'll be here. Sorry for the reluctance on my part—she's very capable and that's not always easy to come by."

"No, it's not." Cillian looked at him pointedly.

Quinn quailed. He gripped the fabric of the couch, his knuckles pale.

"Why are you still sitting here, Quinn? Go."

"But I— What about Beauty?"

"Make sure she's here tomorrow at 9 a.m. sharp."

"So you mean it?"

He's trying to call my bluff. "I do."

"I see." Quinn rose from the couch, avoiding Cillian's gaze. "Well, if there's nothing else—"

"There isn't." He nodded toward the door.

For a moment, it seemed like Quinn would say more. *Please don't let him beg.*

But he didn't. He followed Cillian to the exit then walked slowly away, his head bowed like a man on his way to death. What was it about this Beauty? Was there something going on there? For a moment, his conscience pricked at him.

At the end of the hallway, Quinn turned. "That jewelry— Would it have helped end the war?"

Clearly, the man was a glutton for punishment. But it just wasn't in Cillian to show mercy today. Besides, he could never tell Quinn the truth. "We'll never know, will we?"

THREE

It had *not* been a good day. Despite searching for hours, Beauty and Red had come up empty.

"I just don't understand it. Do you think someone's been violating the decrees and trespassing on our sector?" Like other Guilds, the Hallow Hands marked each street under their jurisdiction, but the white hand that was their symbol didn't mean anything to some of the wilier scavengers. Red stared at the detailed notes in her hand. "According to our calculations, we should've found at least *something* by now."

Beauty held her by the elbow and guided her around a large crack in the rubble-strewn street, stepping over the tough grass clawing its way through as it sought water. *Good luck.* Though Heartcrown was lush with thick, concealing forest, the shield of The Vault prevented any sort of rain, and irrigation was erratic at best. But if rationing water meant the soldiers had more, it was the least they could do. And to tell the truth, the tiny signs of new life gave Beauty hope.. Every time she saw the green tendrils stubbornly growing from blackened remains, the air felt just a little less stale.

"It wouldn't surprise me, even if it is against the law." Before the war, law enforcement had been overseen by Wakelight. With crime nearly nonexistent, the teams of human and robotic officers had been mostly for show. But now that the AI had minimal involvement, the force itself had become unstable and corrupt. Rumors of people being arrested and disappearing swirled through The Vault. Even the transgressions changed daily, the law now a fluid thing governed by a mystery.

And speak of the devil... Beauty held a finger to her lips and pulled Red back around the corner they'd just turned. Shadows fell over the grubby alley, lengthened, paused, then slunk away. Beauty waited a full minute before she let herself breathe again.

Jere believed that Wakelight was more present than The Vault knew, that it had made the force aggressive on purpose so people would keep their heads down and not ask questions—like what was happening outside the wall. Were they winning? Losing? For days, the rest of the Guild had avoided him, as though his traitorous thoughts were contagious. Treason was, after all, a plea to disappear.

They scuttled down narrow side streets until they had no choice but to step onto the main boulevard. Beauty peeked around the wall first, scanning for any signs of danger. Red still had her nose stuck in her map. "Come on." They emerged at the foot of a rise on which stood an ornate building, a lavishly carved dome atop a heavy square base.

Wakelight, and the center of the city. Beauty had loved to climb the grassy hill when she was little, gazing out over the city's sectors from the shadow of their caregiver. Wakelight still existed there, somewhere, though it was no longer concerned with tending to its citizens. How far into ruin would the AI let them go? The banner hanging outside had once proclaimed *A Shining Future for All*. The grimy one there now instead read *Future for the Faithful*.

Beauty sighed. Being faithful wouldn't make a single bit of difference if the war didn't end soon. Every sector of the city would be stripped bare, and they would lose. And if even they won? They'd never be able to rebuild the timeworn stone buildings, now little more than crumbling palaces for the rats who watched with shrewd eyes behind the few shards of glass still clinging to their frames. In fact, the only beauty left in the city was the agricultural sector, its tall vertical gardens practically the sole color in The Vault that wasn't some shade of gray or brown.

"How did we end up *here*?" Red had finally taken her eyes off the map.

"You're the one with the map, not me." If it were up to Beauty, they wouldn't bother with a map; they both knew the city grid by heart. But Red had thought they might be missing some unexplored corner of the artisan sector—the area assigned to the Hallow Hands—where they would find an unspoiled cache.

It was the same story she'd heard whispered in the night market, the one place where all the Guilds sat side-by-side. Every Guild was struggling. Even the agricultural sector was finding it difficult to continue producing. How long could they possibly keep it up?

"Let's just go home." Beauty was tired, dirty, and deflated. "It's getting late." Already the smell of roasting apples drifted on the air; the night market was setting up for business as the dull sky grew even duller. They weren't going to find anything worthwhile today, not without a miracle. And miracles didn't happen in The Vault.

Beauty and Red made it back to the warren
unscathed, as had all the others. Except Father.
He should've returned by now, but perhaps he
and the Beast had more business to talk about,
such as upcoming requisitions. Beauty didn't
want to think about the alternatives.

After Red disappeared to their bedroom to hide
her knife from Kaitlin's thieving fingers, Beauty
found herself alone at the kitchen table with
Violet. The older girl's expression was downcast,
her eyes red-rimmed and shoulders hunched.

"V? Are you okay?" Violet was friendly
enough to Beauty, or had been until she and Arjun
became lost in their own little world.

"I'm fine." Her voice was stiff. *Mind your own
business.*

"Okay." Beauty opened one of the cupboards
and rummaged through the shelves. Red had
baked some biscuits the other day and right now,
they, and a cup of strong chicory, would make the
world right again. *If Jere hasn't found them first.*

"I just don't understand it!"

Violet's outburst caught Beauty by surprise and
her head collided with the cupboard door. "Are
you talking to me?"

"Who else would I be talking to?" the other
girl snapped, her face softening seconds
afterward. "I'm sorry, Beauty, I just—" She
peered around the kitchen, as though expecting
Kaitlin to be hiding in the sugar jar. "Can we
talk?"

"Of course." Beauty gave up trying to find the
biscuits and sat on the bench across from Violet,
rubbing the tender spot on the top of her scalp.
"What's up?"

The other girl wasted no time. "It's Arjun. We've had a fight." She sighed dramatically.

"What about?"

"I don't want to talk about it."

"Okay."

Beauty was halfway out of her seat when Violet grabbed her arm. "Where are you going?"

"You said you didn't want to talk about it."

"That's just what people *say*, Beauty." Her lip trembled.

"I—" She sat back down.

"Well?"

"Well, what?"

"Aren't you going to ask me about it?"

Beauty sighed. "What was the fight about?"

"He should've stood up for me!" Violet slammed her fist on the table.

"What do you mean?"

"With Father. Arjun should've demanded that we get to stay together."

"But Violet, Father could've cast him out. Is that what you want?"

"No, of course not, but...but he should've done it anyway. That's what love is."

It is? Putting yourself in harm's way? But of course she couldn't *say* that. Violet's hand was still balled into a fist. "But Violet, not getting kicked out ensures you get to stay together."

"But it doesn't. When I got angry with him, he told me we should break up. Just like that, like I was nothing."

Beauty searched her heart for sympathy and found none. "It was the right decision, V. If you still love each other after the war, you can be together then, right? You heard what Father said. It's dangerous." In so many ways.

Rachel and Galen. But we don't talk about them.

"So? I don't want to be apart from him, *ever.*"

Ever? Was she ill? It was inconceivable that you would want to be with someone all the time. Beauty loved Red, but she was still glad to have time away from her. Spending twenty-four hours with the same person, day after day? What if they ran out of things to talk about? How did they not annoy the hell out of each other? But of course, they clearly did, or she wouldn't be sitting here right now.

Violet leaned forward and gestured for Beauty to do the same. "I'm thinking of asking him to run away with me." Her voice was hushed.

Had Beauty heard correctly? "Run away?"

"Shh! Do you want everyone else to hear?"

"But, V, you *can't.*"

"Why not?" V stuck out her chin. "We've given everything to this stupid war and I'm sick of it. I don't want to do it anymore."

"Violet, be quiet!" Beauty grabbed her hands. What was with everyone lately? It was *treason.* "You can't talk like that. Not here, not anywhere." And she certainly couldn't run away. It wasn't allowed. She'd—

She'd end up like them. Hung on the hill where Wakelight lived, until even the rats weren't interested anymore.

The chips in their necks might be useless for their original purpose, but they still kept track of where they were at all times. Defectors from the war were not tolerated.

And they shouldn't be.

Galen and Rachel had been selfish. They'd been happy to let everyone keep fighting for their lives, while they tried to hide in the countryside, to live in secret, to *escape*. Escape what? The future? Well, that was exactly what they'd done. And it was right. Victory hung on such a slender thread that they needed to be unified. Any dissidence could not be allowed, or it would spread like the sickness until The Vault fell and they all died at the hands of their enemies.

But Violet was petulant. "Why not? I bet there are ways it could be done. We could remove our chips, and—"

"Violet, you can't! Don't you remember what happened?"

Violet stared at the table; inside Beauty's hands, her palms grew slick. "They weren't careful."

"Yes, they were. Galan was smarter than all of us. They took their chips out. They covered their tracks."

"Then how did they get caught?"

"Someone *told* on them, Violet."

"Who?"

"One of us."

Violet raised her hand to her mouth, and grief clawed at Beauty's heart. This was what love did to you. Any kind of love.

"But who?"

Beauty shook her head. "I don't know for sure. But it's the only way I can think of that they would've been found out. Please, Violet, don't do it. I'm begging you. Just wait until the war is over. Your and Arjun's love will still be there."

"This war will never be over! How long have we been fighting it? Do you even remember the time before the war? Wake up. *Dedication, Duty, Defiance*. Search. *Dedication, Duty, Defiance*. Go to sleep. It's all we do." Her mouth twisted. "What if it *never* ends? Then we'll have spent our entire existence searching through ruins. Our *lives* are ruins." She began crying, loud, ugly, gulping sobs that were sure to bring the others running.

Beauty grabbed her by the wrist and pulled her face close to hers. "Violet. You have to stop this. *Now*. If any of the others hear you—" She left the threat hanging in the scrap of air between them. *Please, let her understand.* If she could calm Violet down now, it might still be okay. *If no one heard her.*

But someone had.

Kaitlin stood in the shadows, her hand on the doorway, her eyes fixed on Violet.

"Kaitlin, Violet's just upset right now. She—"

"I heard everything."

Beauty dropped Violet's hand back on the table and stood. Turning, she squared her shoulders and stalked up to Kaitlin, her heart hammering in her chest. The other girl bared her teeth and held her ground.

"You can't tell anyone what you just heard."

Kaitlin sneered. "I *can*. Maybe I will, maybe I won't."

It was the last straw. "What the hell is wrong with you? Why are you so horrible? You know what will happen if Father or the others find out. She'll be arrested, or worse. Is that what you want?" The desire to punch Kaitlin right in her smirking mouth was almost overwhelming.

Kaitlin laughed. "Oh, calm down. I'm not going to tell anyone."

"You're not?" Suspicion prickled the hairs on the back of Beauty's neck. "Why not?"

"Because I couldn't care less. Let her run away if she wants. More glory for the rest of us. Besides, she's not wrong."

Beauty gaped. Kaitlin had always seemed so dedicated to the cause. *Ruthlessly* dedicated.

"Close your mouth, Beauty."

"But I—"

"What? Thought we were all simpering little disciples like you? *Dedication, Duty, Defiance? Future for the Faithful?* Oh please. I don't care about this stupid war. I just want it to be over, one way or another. All I care about is that *if* we do win, I've gotten enough points to have some kind of decent life afterward."

"I—" How many of them felt this way?

A sigh of despair spun Beauty around. Violet had wilted at the kitchen table, her head in her arms. "Don't ever fall in love, Beauty." She pressed her face into the wood.

"Oh my god, will you please shut up with all the melodrama?" Kaitlin's mouth curled in disgust. There was a racket down the hall as the entrance door flew open. "Besides, I think Father's home."

Father *was* home. Stinking and soaking, an abrasion on his head crusted with blood. Purple bruises were forming on his skin, and he walked with a limp.

"Father!" Beauty rushed up to him, draping his arm across her shoulder as she helped him to the table. "Kaitlin, quick, get the others." But Kaitlin was already sprinting down the hall to the dorms. This was bad. No one had ever dared to attack Father before, not so openly, where everyone else would be able to see.

No one but the Beast.

33

Damn him. Not only had he hurt the man who'd raised her, he'd put the whole Guild in a vulnerable position. If anyone had seen Father making his way home, the word about his weakened state would spread like wildfire.

"Beauty, I'm fine." He batted away her hands. "Leave it."

The others converged on the kitchen. Jere's face was like thunder. "What the hell happened?"

"Father was attacked by the Beast."

Chaos broke out in the room, threats of retribution and violence. Impotent, empty threats.

Only Felix said nothing. He sat down and tied his boots, jerking them so hard that one of the laces snapped.

"Where do you think you're going?" Father winced as he spoke, and a small line of blood welled on his lip.

"Where do you think? I'm going to pay that bastard a visit." Felix stood and patted his pockets.

"Sit down. Nobody's going anywhere." Father nodded as Violet handed him a cloth for his lip.

Felix frowned. "But—"

"I said *sit down.*" It was a command. "You will not be going anywhere near the Beast. Any of you. Now promise me."

Felix refused to meet his eyes.

Father grabbed his arm, his fingers digging into the fabric of his coat. "I said promise me!"

"I promise." Felix jerked his arm away and retreated to the other side of the room to sulk.

"What's the matter with you?" Father turned to Violet. Her eyes were bloodshot, and one of her cuticles was bleeding.

"She was just worried about you, the silly cow." Kaitlin rolled her eyes and took a seat next to Violet. "I told her you'd be fine." She dug her elbow into Violet's ribs and smiled too brightly at her. "I told you he'd be fine. Now you can stop being so ridiculous."

"I really am fine, Violet." This time, Father's voice was kind. He reached out and patted her hand, which only made her choke back another sob.

Kaitlin's smile turned grim and Violet winced.

Beauty kindled the fire and suspended a large pot of water over it. The electricity was out again. They were lucky if they got more than a few hours a day now. They did have a generator, but they used it only to power the security system.

The others—aside from Felix, who had his pride, after all—took a seat at the table, and Beauty joined them as she waited for the water to boil.

"So what happened? Why did the Beast attack you?" Jere spoke brusquely, biting off each word. The attack on Father had clearly shaken him.

Father rubbed his thumb over a welt on the back of his hand. "He wasn't happy with the quality of the jewelry."

Jere exploded. "What? The *quality*? He does realize we're only retrieving the stupid things, not making them, doesn't he? It's an *artifact*." He gripped the edge of the table, his nails gouging the soft wood. "And he beat you for *that*?"

The others murmured their discontent and the tension in the room grew thicker.

Beauty stared at Father, at the way his eyes were downcast, at the pressure he applied to the wound. *He's lying.*

But about what? Clearly, he *had* been attacked.

A.W. Cross

"So what are we going to do about it then?" Felix spoke between gritted teeth. He left his corner and came to stand at Jere's shoulder.

"We're going to do nothing." Father wiped the blood from his skin with determined strokes, keeping his eyes firmly on the cloth.

"Why not? He can't treat us this way. I don't give a damn about his reputation. We can take him."

"It's not that simple, Felix. It's not about whether we could beat him in a fight. He's our only link to the outside world right now. The way we deal with him will impact our future when the war is over. Do you really want to jeopardize that over a couple of bumps and bruises?"

"So that's it? We just let him treat us however he wants?"

"For now, yes. We play nice."

"But how far will it go?" Kaitlin's expression was calculating. "If he gets away with this, what will he do the next time?"

"It doesn't matter." Father sighed and dropped the cloth on the table. "We have to be smart, pick our battles as we always have. This is no exception."

Beauty glanced around the table. He was losing them. They'd made their reputation by being smart, cunning, and ruthless. This was the first time Father had ever shown them weakness.

He sensed it as well. "Look, think of it as a long game. We bide our time—for now. When the war is over, he loses that position of power over us. Then," he mustered a wicked grin, "we remind him of what he did, and we take care of it."

There was silence until Jere leaned back from the table and shrugged. "That's different. I can live with that. As long as he's not going to go unpunished." The others murmured in agreement, mollified. Only Felix continued to glower. But he would come around; he always did.

Beauty rose from the table and pulled a mug out of the cupboard. At least Father was home safely. Hopefully, what had happened would distract him from her and Red's disastrous day. It was a selfish thought, when he sat there bruised and bloody, but she was too tired and disheartened to bear the irritation in his eyes. Or worse, the disappointment. She was already disappointed enough. Not a single contribution today to help end the war. If it did drag on forever, like Violet said, it would be partly her fault.

Dedication, Duty, Defiance.

She sighed. Tomorrow would be a better day. It had to be.

As she poured steaming water over the chicory in the bottom of the mug, Father spoke again.

"There's more."

The uneasiness that had plagued Beauty throughout the day deepened, sinking into her very bones.

"Beauty, please sit down."

Her mind rebelled. *Don't sit. If you do, whatever it is will become true.* But her body, used to obeying commands, sat, the mug she'd prepared for him clutched in her hands.

"We have to replace what was...unacceptable."

That's it? Beauty breathed a sigh of relief. So why, then, did he look so tense? Artifacts like jewelry were difficult to come by, but not impossible. They could do it in a day if they all worked together.

"Beauty, the Beast has demanded you in reparation."

The mug shattered. Scalding water gushed between her fingers, the pain so intense that, for a moment, she felt nothing. Then came a fire, hot and all-consuming, and the room spun before her eyes.

"Beauty!" Small hands wrapped around her shoulders, pulling her from the bench and over to the sink. Red. She turned the cold faucet on full blast and plunged Beauty's hands all the way to the bottom, pressing them against the cold steel. "Breathe, Beauty."

But she couldn't. She couldn't make sense of what was happening. The Beast. Pain. They melded together in her mind, and somewhere, far away, someone screamed.

"Quick, give her this." A new pain, a sting in her arm. And then...numbness. Her hands still hurt, but the fire had cooled to a low burn. Distant, no longer hers.

"Beauty, sit down."

As the drugs coursed through her veins, the shapeless fire in her mind tempered, sharpening her wits.

"What do you mean you gave me to the Beast?" The sound came from her mouth, but the voice was too strong, too steady to be hers.

The Beast. The brute who'd beaten her father. Who held their future in his inhuman hands. The monster.

"I didn't *give* you to him, Beauty. Of course not." But his guilty expression said otherwise. "It's just temporary, to make up for what happened. You're just going to work as his assistant for a bit."

"So I get to come home at night?" That wasn't so bad. She would bear it, for his sake.

"Well, no. I— You have to stay there with him, for as long as he needs you."

Stay there. For as long as he needs you. "So you sold me."

"No, I—"

"Yes, you did! I thought— I thought—" *What? That Father cared about you? That you were important? That he loved you?* He'd said himself that love was dangerous. She'd just been too stupid to think that included her. But he'd never cared about her for anything more than what she could bring him.

Fine.

She struggled to her feet, weaving slightly, still lightheaded from the pain and the drugs. Her hands throbbed as she pushed him away when he tried to comfort her. "Get away from me. I'll go."

"You will?" The relief in his eyes was the final betrayal.

"Guess you're not the favorite anymore." But Kaitlin's dark eyes were fixed on Father.

Beauty turned and ran. Blinded by tears, she found her way to her bed by painful touch. A few minutes later, the door opened softly. "Go away. I hate you."

"It's me, Beauty." *Red.* He couldn't even come after her. He was a coward. A traitor. A liar. He wasn't her father. She would never call him that again. *You told Violet that Arjun letting her go was the safest thing. What else was Fa—Raphael to do?* But still it stung, even worse than her scalded hands.

The bed sank as Red sat next her and put a hand on her blanket-covered head. "Beauty, what are you going to do?"

"I'm going to go to the Beast."

"But you can't. You—" Red sought her hand under the blanket and Beauty winced as her fingers brushed the scalded skin. "Oops. Sorry."

"I can't stay here. Not after what...Raphael did." If Red noticed the change, she didn't comment.

"But the *Beast*? What if he hurts you? Or worse?"

With a yelp, Beauty yanked the blanket off and glared at Red. "So what? I don't care anymore."

"You don't mean that."

"I do!" But Red was right, and they both knew it.

Red gave her a wan smile. "Maybe it won't be so bad."

"You never were a good liar, either."

Red bit her lip. "Beauty, promise me: if he does anything to hurt you, you'll escape. You'll come find me and we'll...I don't know, run away."

"Where would we go?"

"I don't know. Down to the sea? We can find a cave to hide in, and we'll spend our days fishing."

"And wear dresses made of seaweed."

"And sleep in."

They grinned at each other, and Beauty's heart cracked. They would never run away. They would never live on the beach. Tomorrow, Red would get up and go on the hunt, as she did every day. She would think about Beauty, but nothing more. And each day she would think of her less and less, until she was like Rachael and Galen, little more than a memory and a whisper in the dark. And Raphael would take Beauty to the Beast, and leave her at his mercy, when they all knew he had none.

Red lay down next to Beauty, and they spent their final night as sisters did, side by side, their arms linked. A few hours before dawn, Beauty finally slept, her dreams haunted by a dark presence, black of heart and sharp of teeth. And yet, there was comfort in that darkness, a soothing voice, a gentle hand. In circles, she ran, away from the presence yet always back to it, around and around, until she was exhausted and woke, her body covered in sweat and the pain in her hands ignited.

Red stirred next to her, and Beauty remembered. *The Beast.*

Looked like today wouldn't be a good day either.

FOUR

It was a huge mistake. What had he been thinking? How could he have let Cybel make him think this was a good idea, even for a second?

It's not Cybel's fault. He had to make an example of Quinn for the others. *You also wanted to spite him. You have no one to blame but your pride.*

Well, he might've made the mistake, but he didn't have to prolong it any more than necessary. He'd keep this Beauty for a couple of days, just long enough to show Quinn and the others he meant business—for he knew damn well that if the other Guilds hadn't heard about it already, they would soon—then he would send her back, and look merciful. It would keep the scavengers on their toes. Still, next time he was going to have to try harder to control his temper.

"What do you think she's going to be like?" Cybel twirled on her wheels. If the Beast hadn't known any better, he'd have thought she was excited.

She. He'd always thought of Cybel as a she.

That's what the isolation does to you. Did robots even have a gender?

His loneliness was self-imposed, of course. He could easily make his presence in The Vault more obvious, like his counterparts in the other city sectors. But it would only put the truth—the truth only he knew—at risk.

Admit it, you actually have a conscience—not that it does you any good. You're still a coward.

He pressed his fingers over his eyes, as though he could push the thoughts away. They'd been surfacing more and more lately, and they were dangerous.

"I'm going to regret this, aren't I?"

"Why?"

"You know damn well why. Next time, do me a favor and don't make suggestions that my pride can't ignore."

"I think it's a good idea. It's lonely down here, just the two of us."

"Lonely? You're a robot. How can you be lonely? Besides, what about me?" For some reason, her loneliness bothered him. Wasn't he good enough company?

Cybel gave a tinny laugh. "You're not exactly a great conversationalist. Besides, all your brooding and angst can be a bit of a downer."

"A *downer?* What could you possibly know about—" The security alert sounded.

"Ooh, they're here!" Cybel spun in a circle then sped toward the door.

The Beast braced himself. *Let's get this over with. Just let her in, be the Beast for a few minutes then hand her over to Cybel and get the hell out.*

"Remember, Cybel, she's your responsibility."

"I know." The little robot's voice was thrilled.

He stared at the couple on the screen. The expression on Quinn's face was a mix of emotions—

anger, shame, regret. Well, he should've been more careful.

His protégé's feelings were more difficult to read. She stood straight, her shoulders back and chin up. Her fists, wrapped in white bandages, were clenched at her sides.

Is she fantasizing about using them on me?

She looked younger than he'd expected, uncommon in The Vault. Living under the constant threat of war tended to prematurely age a person, instilling an unconscious awareness that was eternally exhausting, even if you weren't aware of it. That he knew firsthand. Besides, she'd probably been up all night wondering about the cruelties the horrible Beast was going to subject her to.

She raised a bandaged hand and tugged it through her hair then smoothed the homespun coat she wore, as though concerned about how she looked. Then she seemed to realize what she was doing and snatched her hands away. Did she think that would make a difference? Horror struck him. Did she think he would...

Well, he wouldn't. He would *never*. Was that something she had to worry about in The Vault? The thought of vicious hands knotting themselves in that glossy brown hair, bringing fear to her delicate face, filled him with a rage he hadn't felt since the battlefield. If he ever heard of such a thing going on in his sector...they would come to know the real meaning of his nickname. And what the hell had happened to her hands? Had she tried to do something to herself, hoping to sour the deal?

He opened the door. In watching her, he'd forgotten himself. Forgotten the effect he had on people.

She clapped both hands over her mouth, but it did little to stifle her scream. Tears squeezed from the corners of her eyes and she swayed where she stood.

Any gentle feelings he'd had toward her vanished. To her, he was nothing but a monster. Like every other person he'd met, she couldn't see past the way he looked.

Why did you expect her to be any different? And more importantly, why does it bother you? You only brought her here to prove a point to Quinn.

He peered down at her through the mask, grateful, as always, that his expression was hidden. "Are you done?" He kept his voice neutral.

She started at the sound, as though she'd expected something less human.

"Well?"

She took a deep breath and raised her chin. "Yes."

"Good. Come inside." As she stepped through the doorway, he began to close the door behind her. "Goodbye, Quinn."

Quinn took a step forward, his face contorting in surprise. Had he still thought it all a bluff? That he could show up and the Beast would simply take it as a sign of his loyalty and dismiss them both with a warning? In truth, the Beast was sorely tempted, but no, he had to see this through. He splayed a hand on Quinn's chest, the soft flesh yielding under the metal, and stopped him in his tracks. "Go."

"But I—"

"Relinquished her to my care."

"Not that you gave him a choice." Her voice shook slightly as she spoke to Cillian, but her eyes were dry. Her composure was admirable.

Quinn, on the other hand, looked like she'd slapped him. "Beauty, I— I'm sorry." He grasped for her. "I'm sorry."

She stepped out of reach. "Go. Before he decides I'm not high quality enough either and demands even more."

Quinn looked away.

He didn't tell her the truth.

Cillian narrowed his eyes at the other man, and Quinn shook himself. "I—" He raised his hands again then let them fall as she ignored him. "Take care of yourself."

She nodded curtly then spun and marched past Cillian, taking obvious care not to touch him.

As Cillian moved to close the door behind them, Quinn put his foot in the gap. "Look—"

The Beast kicked his boot free and shut the door in his face.

He found Beauty at the end of the hall.

"The door is locked." Her eyes burned into him.

"Yes. Security."

"Have a lot of enemies, do you?" Her tone was sharp, but as he glanced at her, she dropped her eyes.

"Something like that." He paused. She'd brought a scent with her, something familiar. Something soothing and distracting at the same time.

She mumbled something under her breath, but he didn't catch it. He pressed his palm to the pad on the wall and the door slid open.

She stayed in the hallway, wary. "Where are we going?"

He ignored her and went into the next room, leaving her to trail behind him. Best just to give her a quick tour then leave her to Cybel.

The robot waited on the other side of the door, practically vibrating with excitement.

The Beast gestured to her. "Beauty, this is—"

Cybel rolled forward, pushing past him. "Cybel. Pleased to meet you."

Beauty looked down at the little robot and broke into a smile. It transformed her face, as though a layer of grime had washed away.

How long had it been since he'd seen someone smile? People didn't usually smile at him in his line of work, unless you counted nervous grins. When was the last time *he'd* smiled, for that matter? Could he even remember how?

"It's nice to meet you. I—"

"You'll be working with Cybel while you're here. She'll show you where everything is, explain what we do. Mostly, you'll be sorting and archiving deliveries then preparing items for shipment when and as they're needed."

The smile dropped from her face, a shadow falling over it once more. "Whatever helps the cause. That's the only reason I agreed to come."

The cause. Damn the cause. "Quinn gave you a choice, did he?"

She colored. "No, but—"

"He must've been very distraught, having to give up one of his wards to the Beast."

Her lip trembled, but still she didn't cry.

He was relentless. "That's the reason you're here, Beauty, because of him. Not for the cause. He gave you up to save his own ass." The words were like salt in his mouth. *I'm so tired of being the enemy.*

"I don't believe you."

He shrugged. "You don't have to." He turned away from her. "Cybel will also show you where you can and can't go. You do as you're told, and everything will be fine."

"Or what? You'll beat me? Kill me?" Her voice trembled.

A bitter laugh forced its way from his throat.

At the sound, the self-control that had carried her so far finally slipped. "Like you killed Stiles? Like you beat Raphael, just because you didn't like what he'd brought you, what you'd *ordered* him to bring you?" She took a step toward him, her body quivering with anger. Impressive, but futile. He was made of metal and towered over her by more than a foot and a half.

But what the hell was she talking about? Stiles? The man had been ill for a year, though he'd hidden it well. And as for Quinn... It came together in his mind suddenly. "You think I *killed* Stiles? And beat Quinn?"

Her hands curled into fists. "Don't try to deny it."

"I don't need to try. I'm flat-out denying it."

"Then what happened to them?"

"Stiles was killed by residual damage from the sickness. His lungs finally gave out. As for Quinn..." He hesitated. Exposing Quinn for the coward he was suddenly felt wrong. But he couldn't let her think that he— *What? Really are a monster?* Pride and frustration bit at him again.

"I didn't beat him. He'd already been attacked when he got here."

"You're a liar. Why wouldn't he tell us that? Why would he let us think you hurt him?"

"Because it makes him look better than the truth?"

48

"I don't know what that means. All I know is that he came home, battered and bloody, and the next thing I know I have to come here and—" She flew at him suddenly, her hands raised to strike him. What did she think she was doing?

There was a sharp crack as her bandaged fist connected with the metal plate of his chest. Agony flashed across her face and yet she drew her fist back again, preparing to land another blow.

Cillian grabbed her wrists, holding them in an unyielding vise.

She struggled against him for a moment then settled for screaming up into his face instead. "You're a monster. A horrible monster, and I hate you. I hate—"

"Why don't you show her the truth?" Cybel's voice was soft, but it cut through Beauty's rage like a knife. She screamed wordlessly at him one more time then sagged to the floor.

"What's the truth?" Her voice broke over the last word, and Cillian wished he could go back in time to yesterday and punch the Beast that had demanded Quinn bring her here. The situation just kept getting worse.

"Nothing. It's—"

"Show her, C—"

"Cybel. Stop. It's not important."

"How can you say that? I won't have her thinking such things about you. If you don't show her, I will."

He would've laughed at the prim disapproval of her tone if there hadn't been a young woman shaking around his ankles. "Fine." There was no point arguing with Cybel. If he didn't show Beauty the truth, the robot would eventually. He had to expose Quinn or send her home now. He sighed. The truth would be painful to her, but it was better than living a lie.

You're a hypocrite of the worst kind.

He ignored the voice. "Get up."

She glared at him from the floor. Was she going to be contrary about everything?

"If you want to know the truth, get up. Otherwise, you can sleep there."

She held his gaze for a moment longer then climbed to her feet, wincing as her hands pushed off from the floor. Once standing, she refused to look at him.

"What happened to your hands?"

"Why do you care?"

She was exasperating. "I don't." He turned from her and began walking toward the control room.

After a moment's pause, she followed him. "I scalded them. When I—"

"Watch this." He replayed the recording of Quinn and his visit the day before, watching Beauty's face as Raphael, clearly intoxicated, stumbled down the corridor, his hands scrabbling at the wall for support. Blood darkened his head and hands, and he walked with a limp that wasn't solely the result of alcohol.

It was only then that Beauty began to cry. The tears fell silently, her face still as she watched the man who'd raised her become fallible.

"He lied to us. To me." The fight had gone out of her, replaced by an acceptance painful to see. He knew the feeling well, watching everything you thought to be true crumble before your eyes, thanks to the selfishness of those supposed to protect you.

"Come on." He led her to what passed as their living room. After maneuvering her gently down, he retreated to the other side of the room to lean awkwardly against the wall.

"What happened?" Her voice was thin, as though she couldn't draw in enough breath, despite the rapid rise and fall of her chest.

"He got drunk on Demon's Breath on his way here and was robbed."

"But why would he— What he was carrying was so precious."

"I—"

Her face turned hard a second time. "It's your fault."

What? *Again?* How was it his fault after what he'd just shown her?

"He's terrified of you. We all are. No wonder he had to get drunk to come and see you. He thought you'd killed Stiles."

"Well, I didn't. Don't believe everything you're told." *Just go, Cillian. She doesn't care about the truth. And why do you care what she thinks, anyway?*

"But you hurt people. You make them fear you. You—"

He'd had enough. "Do you ever think for yourself?"

That took her aback. Her chin shot up and she scowled at him. "Of course I do. I—"

"It doesn't seem like it. It seems to me you're just parroting the same old crap as everyone else, with no evidence to prove it."

"It's true," Cybel piped up. "I wouldn't allow him to behave so badly."

"You—" He rounded on Cybel. "You—" He gave up, throwing his hands in the air. This was

51

pointless. All he was going to do was make himself feel worse. And like a fool, for trying to explain. "Think what you want. All I've done is try to tell you the truth."

Or some of it, anyway. But what's one less lie? Do you really think it makes a difference? You're still a monster.

He turned to leave.

"Wait."

He stopped in the doorway and looked back over his shoulder.

This time, Beauty held his gaze. "I'm sorry. I—"

"It doesn't matter. Get some sleep." He turned away again. "Cybel will show you to your room." It came out harsher than he'd intended, but he didn't look back. He couldn't. Not after she'd apologized. It was what he'd wanted, and yet it brought no relief. He almost wished she was angry again, or seething with resentment. Anything but the defeat he'd just read so clearly on her face.

He didn't want to answer any of the questions he knew were coming. *Why would he lie to me? Why would he take such a risk? How could he just give me away, like I'm nothing?* The questions he'd have asked if he'd been in her position. Again, he cursed the war. What was the purpose of fighting if people had gotten to the point where they were now sacrificing their loved ones? Quinn clearly believed the hype about the Beast—even though his own punishment could've been much worse—yet, he'd still given Beauty, someone supposedly precious, up to him. He should've taken her place, protected her.

Where do you get off being so self-righteous? You're no better than he is.

But he could be.

In that moment, something inside him changed, and the seed of a plan formed. From now on, there would be no looking back. For either of them.

"Oh, and Cybel? Give her something for her hands." He shut the door behind him.

FIVE

Why did he lie to me? How could he lie to me?

Beauty lay in the dark, in the strange bed in the unfamiliar room, filled with unwelcome thoughts. She hadn't really believed that Raphael would leave her here, with the Beast.

The Beast wasn't the one who lied to you.

She pushed the thought away...but in the dark and the silence, she eventually couldn't avoid it any longer.

Why let me think the Beast had beaten him on a whim?

Surely, he knew the truth would come out sooner or later?

Of course he did. He doesn't expect you to come back. He's sent you into the lion's den and left you for dead.

She'd thought she knew him. That he'd cared for her. Loved her like a father. But fathers weren't supposed to discard their daughters.

And now she was alone, orphaned and abandoned. Again. Even if the Beast let her go, she couldn't return to the Guild. She'd never be able to look at Raphael the same way, to hold her tongue and say nothing. What did the others think about her exile? Did they even care? Or were they glad the favorite was finally gone? She gave a bitter snort. Well, if she had been his favorite, the rest of them had better watch out.

So what could she do now? Surely she couldn't stay here with the Beast. What if she made him angry? What would happen to her then?

When he'd opened the door, she hadn't been able to stifle her gasp. All the rumors spoke about his metal face and covered hands... Many wondered if he was human at all. She shivered with revulsion. Any human augmentation but their issued chips was considered abomination in Heartcrown and had been as long as she could remember. So was the costume he wore—the gloves, the hood, the mask— just another way to provoke fear and obedience?

The mask was the most curious of all. The rumors had described it as the face of a demon. In fact, it had almost no features at all, smooth, and inhuman, with only the suggestion of a nose, and a cruel, thin slit for a mouth. So yes, it was the face of a monster, but there was a man in there somewhere too.

"Are you okay?" a small voice asked beside her.

She rolled over. Cybel stood next to the bed. Non-humanoid robots were familiar in Heartcrown, but had been relatively uncommon in Wakelight, even before the war. And despite her misery, Beauty was fascinated by the little figure. Her paneled torso was vaguely human-shaped, but rather than legs, she sported a wider column flanked by two large wheels. Her head was a small white sphere encased in a wide black band from which two blue-glowing eyes peered curiously at Beauty. Her little arms were raised as though unsure whether to reach out and comfort Beauty, or show she meant no harm.

"I'm—" She began to cry again. She couldn't help it. If Cybel had just left her alone, she would've made it through the night okay, overwhelmed into numbness. But that simple question, an act of kindness, was the last straw, and her chest heaved painfully as she gasped and sobbed.

When she finally stopped, Cybel still stood by the bed, watching her. "Did that help?"

"No. Yes. I don't know." Beauty was drained, hollow.

"I have something for your hands." The bot held up a small container.

"What is it?"

"A salve. Here, let me help you." Before Beauty could speak, Cybel unwound the bandages, making oddly human sounds of sympathy as she went. "He's not so bad, you know."

"Who? Raphael or the Beast?"

"C— The Beast."

Beauty hissed as the air hit her blistered skin. "Why is he so horrible?"

"Is he?"

"Yes, he—" He what, exactly? The only firsthand account she'd had of his violent nature was from Raphael—and he'd lied.

Cybel waited patiently, her small fingers rubbing the salve so gently onto Beauty's burns that it was almost soothing. The scent of the salve was from before the war, a deeply floral aroma.

"Okay, well, if he's not so terrible, why does everyone think he is?"

"Because he has power over them." She wrapped fresh white bandages over the salve-covered skin.

"And he's never done anything violent?"

"I didn't say that. But when he has, he's had good reason. His position here isn't easy. He's sacrificed a lot."

"Who hasn't? That's no excuse to dress like a monster and go around terrifying people."

"He's lost more than most."

"What do you mean? In the war?"

"It's not my story to tell. What I can tell you is to not be deceived by appearances. He may look monstrous, and at times he may even *be* monstrous, but his heart is anything but."

Can it be true?

Beauty had never heard such sentiment from a robot before. What kind of robot was she? None of the other bots she'd seen in The Vault were so...articulate. Or seemingly sentient, for that matter. One more mystery. *He probably programmed her to say that.* That had to be it.

Cybel patted her arm. "I'll change the bandages again tomorrow. Is there anything else you need?"

Beauty glanced down at her neatly wrapped hands. Whatever was in that salve was working its magic. The throbbing sting was gone, in its place only a comforting warmth. Drained and finally free of hours of pain, Beauty could no longer resist the desire to sleep creeping over her. Whatever mysteries the Beast and Cybel held, tomorrow would be soon enough to uncover them.

* * *

When Beauty woke the next morning, little metal fingers were still nestled between her bandaged hands. Had Cybel stayed with her all night? She peered over the edge of the bed to thank her and found an empty space.

The hand was *just* a hand. Beauty yelped in surprise and dropped it.

At the sound of the metal hitting the floor, Cybel rolled into the room. "Oh, sorry. Did that startle you? I needed to go finish up some jobs, but you'd held on so tightly all night long, I didn't want to disturb you."

So she'd taken off her hand? That was...weird. But sweet, too, in a way.

"Thank you."

"What do young women eat for breakfast? We have a big day ahead of us, so you'll need your energy."

"Oh. Um, porridge, mostly."

"One porridge coming up." How was it possible for her to sound so cheerful?

"Will...the Beast be joining us?" After her conversation with Cybel last night, Beauty found herself curious to see him again.

"No. He's already had his breakfast and gone to take care of some business."

"What does *he* eat for breakfast?"

"Children, mostly, but today he just had some bread."

Beauty stared at Cybel. Was she joking? The little robot bustled back and forth, and in only a few minutes, a steaming bowl of porridge was shoved under Beauty's nose. "There you go."

"Thank you."

When Beauty had finished eating, Cybel took her on a tour of her new home.

"It's huge." It was the largest underground space Beauty had ever been in, a vast cavern with a high, curved ceiling hewn into the rock. Off the central room were wide corridors leading into further chambers. And each room was filled with some of the most incredible objects Beauty had ever seen.

"Go, have a look for yourself." Cybel followed her, seemingly proud of the collection. And she should've been. The Guild rarely advertised the things they'd found, and Beauty could understand why. The items in these rooms represented a fortune. Statues, works of art, precious stones, and metals...

"I'm surprised so much of it's kept here." She traced her finger over the thigh of a particularly curvy statue. "I would've thought everything would be shipped out right away. I mean, wars are expensive, right?"

"We ship them out as required."

Required by whom? And *where* did they go? The Guilds never knew exactly what happened to their contributions. "Where—" They entered the next room.

It was full of books.

They lined the walls from floor to ceiling, more spilling out of boxes placed around the room. In the center of the small chamber was a low table and a big, shabby armchair.

Cybel peered up at her. "You like books?"

"I *love* books. I read all the time."

As Beauty ran her fingers over the titles, reciting them in her head, a pattern emerged. "Hey...a lot of these are books *I* recovered. I'd have thought they'd be long gone by now."

"Not much call for books these days."

"But the soldiers... Don't they—"

"Let's keep moving." As they walked past the low table, something shiny caught Beauty's eye. On the glossy surface lay a golden locket, a delicate rose engraved on the front.

"It's beautiful. Whose is this?" She held the jewelry out to Cybel.

The robot studied it. "Hmm. I'm not sure. But why don't you just keep it? Think of it as a welcome gift."

"Keep it? Really?"

"Yeah, why not? It won't be missed."

Beauty undid the clasp holding the locket closed. Inside was a picture of a young man, grinning confidently at the camera. His black hair was close-cropped, and his brown eyes glittered with mischief.

"Whose picture is this?" She turned it toward Cybel.

The robot barely glanced at it. "Who knows? Any one of the million who used to live in Wakelight."

Whoever the young man was, Beauty was drawn to him and to the mystery of his identity. It was a tragic, romantic kind of mystery—just the sort she loved to read about.

"Thank you." She tucked it away in her pocket.

It was the most valuable thing she'd ever owned. They'd never been allowed to keep anything they found in the ruins, Raphael even going so far as to scan them each night, just in case they'd forgotten to completely empty their pockets. It was for their own safety, he'd said. And anything her parents may have left her had disappeared before she'd even known about it.

The necklace felt heavy in her pocket as she followed Cybel through the rest of the Beast's cave. She continued to marvel at all she saw, but her mind kept returning to her new secret. Still, she left it untouched until late that evening, when she'd finally gone to bed. Only once she'd assured Cybel that she was fine, that the robot didn't need to stay with her another night, did she pull it out and unclasp it, peering at it in the dim light.

Who was he? She would never know. But she could pretend. He was a prince, she decided, of a faraway land. A prince of a country no one would dare to invade, too strong to fall to its enemies. Children were born, grew up with their families, played, went to school. They didn't sacrifice their lives digging through ruins until their fingernails were splintered and their skin torn. They didn't have to look over their shoulders every step of the way home. Their fathers hugged them close with love, not because of what they could scavenge. They didn't give their children away to beasts.

He wasn't a beast, this prince. He was kind and handsome. *Very* handsome. She touched his face with her pinkie finger. He smiled easily, and laughed, and read books, and...was probably dead.

And so was the one the locket had been intended for.

Beauty dropped the jewelry on the bed as though it had burned her. What was she doing? He wasn't a prince. There was no such thing. And this locket was only yet another fragment of a life that would never again exist. Grief welled inside her for the young man, and for herself. Before today, Beauty had always looked forward, into the future that would one day come when the war was over. But what if Violet was right, what if that day never came? This young man, whoever he was, would stay forgotten, as though he'd never existed.

Well, not if she could help it. She couldn't save him, but she could bear witness. Even if no one else ever knew him or remembered him, *she* would. She put the locket around her neck. The chain was longer than normal, the oval pendant falling over her heart.

She pressed it to her skin hard enough to make a mark and promised him: *I see you. I will carry you with me always, and when this war is over, I will find out who you were, and I will remember you.*

SIX

Slowly over the next week, Beauty began to relax. If she hadn't been sent to live with a so-called monster to pay for the sins of her father, it would've been almost pleasant. The dread that had filled her on her arrival, that had dogged her through that first night and each night thereafter, faded, and she began to look forward to each day spent with Cybel.

They had fallen easily into a routine. Every morning after breakfast, the Beast would give them their daily task. Sometimes they were to sort the items that had been delivered to him the previous day. This was Beauty's favorite task. A thrill of anticipation rushed up her spine every time he indicated, in his brusque way, a new shipment of crates draped with canvas tarping. It was like all the best parts of her old job, but without any of the risk—both of coming home empty-handed or being robbed on the way.

Every time, she held her breath as Cybel opened the cargo, trying to guess what treasures would be inside, and today's shipment was no different. There were more crates than usual, so she decided to help Cybel out.

As her fingers grazed the studded wood, she found herself flat on her back, her skin tingling and her feet burning like she'd stood in a fire. Her hands, still healing, throbbed in sympathy.

"Beauty!" The bot tilted over her, the light of her eyes flashing with warning.

She coughed as she pushed herself onto her elbows. "What happened?"

"I'm so sorry. I shocked you."

"You *shocked* me? Why would you do that?" She struggled to sit up, her joints seeming to crackle with energy.

"You must never open a box until I scan it, Beauty. Never, *never*."

"Why not?"

"Because... The Beast is not well-loved."

What a surprise. "So?"

"So, sometimes there are things in those boxes. Things that could kill you."

"People try to kill him?"

Yes, he was the Beast, but surely people realized that hurting him would only damage the war effort? When the agricultural sector had risen up against their liaison, their crops had rotted in the field for weeks, an unconscionable loss. And the woman who replaced him was even more demanding.

But it's easy to forget the consequences when you live in fear.

"Maybe he should try to be less...beastly to people."

"He has his reasons," Cybel replied tartly. "Besides, that's not why they try to hurt him. They think that if they can remove him, they will take his place."

"Would that be so bad?"

"He may be many things, and not all of them pleasant, but he isn't a thief. Everything he collects here goes where it's supposed to. Can you say the same of the people you know? People like your...father?"

"He's not my father. Not anymore." But Cybel was right. If the Guild had this much wealth sitting in their care, they would make sure the majority of it went to the right place, of course, but having spent so much time working for a life after the war, skimming off the top would've been seen as nothing more than investing in one's future. She hated to admit it, but it was true. Even she would've done it.

She dusted herself off. "I'll be more careful from now on."

"Good. Come on. We have to get a shipment ready." Cybel rolled off toward the room that housed the antiquities.

"Where does everything *go*?" Beauty had asked this before and still hadn't gotten a straight answer from the robot. "I mean, I know they go to support the war effort, but where do they actually go to do that? How do they get there?"

"He takes them."

"I know, but *where*?"

"It doesn't matter."

Beauty opened her mouth to press her on the subject, but the little robot rolled away, mumbling about an urgent task. *Why is she so reluctant to talk about it?* Normally, Cybel chattered away almost continually. She must've been lonely before Beauty arrived, for the Beast didn't speak much. At least, not when Beauty was around.

The Beast. She'd expected to be working under his baleful glare, and so for the first few nights had gone to sleep with a knot of dread in her belly, and the lines of his mask etched into her mind. But each morning after his cursory instructions, she rarely saw him again before the next morning. Was he staying away on purpose? Part of her was relieved, but another part, albeit a smaller part, was disappointed. Now that she'd gotten over her initial fear of him, her curiosity had only increased. He had been different with Raphael, all seething power laced with the promise of violence. With her, he was gruff, true, and he didn't make idle conversation, but on the rare times Beauty had seen him during the day, and had asked him about a particular item, he'd become animated, the Beast forgotten, *especially* when the conversation was about books. He seemed to love books almost as much as she did.

After the first night, Beauty had retreated to the room that housed the books, hoping they would ease her fear. They had, and she'd begun to make a habit of it. She called it the library in her head, and she could barely wait to finish her supper each night so she could go and lose herself for the few hours left before bedtime. Cybel didn't care much for books, and in truth, Beauty appreciated the solitude. It was a luxury after a life lived in such close proximity to others. She'd never even had her own room before, and now she had not only a bedroom, but her own personal library.

On her third night, she'd settled into an old armchair, a smaller version of the one already there. She'd dragged it over from what Cybel had christened the 'junk room'—where they housed the items that weren't worth anything but still showed up at their door every few days. Cybel said they were from people who were struggling to find objects of worth but were still desperate to maintain their standing in The Vault.

"That must make him furious."

"It doesn't. He understands. He sometimes adds any surplus items to their accounts."

Who was this empathetic man Cybel seemed to worship? Was it the robot's programming, or was he really not the monster everyone made him out to be? The only way to know for sure was for Beauty to spend some time with him, outside of the orders he'd given her.

Hence the second chair. She'd pulled it up to the other side of the low table. The larger chair likely meant he came here to read as she did, and if there were *two* chairs, perhaps he would join her.

Her plan finally paid off. One night, she sat absorbed in a tale of adventure, danger, and romance, when the Beast came into the library. He didn't notice her at first behind the high back of the chair, and she watched him scan the shelves for a few minutes until he pulled one free and turned around. If he was startled to see her, he didn't show it, and disappointment leached some of the anticipation from her surprise. To mask it, she gestured to the second chair a few feet away from hers. "Will you join me?"

That seemed to surprise him. He glanced between her and his chair, hesitating, and for a moment, it seemed as though he would turn on his heel and walk away. Instead, to her satisfaction, he eased himself down into the chair. He sat awkwardly at first, perched on the edge, but as Beauty returned to her book and didn't press him for conversation, he settled back and opened his own.

Beauty stole glances at him out of the corner of her eye. She had so many questions she didn't dare ask Cybel. Why did he still wear the mask around her? Surely they'd gotten past the point of his charade by now? It must be stifling under there. Why didn't he just take it off? Or was there more to it than that? Was there something under there he didn't want her to see?

Her imagination wouldn't rest, running in circles in her head and making it impossible for her to concentrate on her book. When she laid awake at night, gazing at the young man in the locket, a story had begun to form; she couldn't help it. She told herself that the Beast was the handsome prince's evil brother, that he'd been banished from their kingdom to The Vault as punishment for his crimes. There he ruled over the people with darkness and fear, but one day, his golden brother would come and liberate them all, including her. He would fall in love with her the minute he laid eyes on her, and she would become a princess. He would carry her far away from here, to a land where no war existed. But now, watching the Beast reading next to her, the story sounded ridiculous.

He'd come again the next night, and each night after that. They spent the evenings in silence, he absorbed in his book, and Beauty absorbed in her curiosity. Once or twice, he caught her staring at him and, face burning, she lowered her eyes to her own book, determined not to look at him again. But she always did.

"Yes?" His voice startled her. She'd been staring again.

"Nothing. Just wondering what you're reading."

He leaned over, his eyes shining oddly in the low light. "You?"

She showed him the cover.

"A romance?"

She nodded. "I've read it a hundred times. It's one of my favorites." It was impossible to read his expression behind the mask. Was that a note of amusement in his voice? Was he laughing at her? Of course he was. He probably thought she was just another silly girl.

"Don't they die of grief at the end?"

"Yes, but—"

He pointed at the stack of books she'd piled on the table between them, tapping the spines as he went. "Suicide. One hung and the other dies of grief. Dies in childbirth. Suicide. Drowns." He peered at her. "A bit grim, don't you think?"

"You've read all of these? You *like* romance novels?"

"I've *read* them. I don't know that I like them."

"Why not?"

He shrugged. "They never seem to end well. Don't you think a romance should have a happy ending?"

"I—"

"I mean, what's the point otherwise? To go through all that heartache for nothing? Doesn't make love very appealing." He shrugged. "Mind you, I suppose a tragic ending is closer to real life."

Hopefully, he couldn't see her blush in the dim light. "What are *you* reading?"

He held up the volume for her to see. A book on war. "Ends about the same as your books." His tone was dry.

"Do you think the war will end soon?" Since he actually seemed to be open to conversation, Beauty seized the moment. Maybe she could find out more about him.

"No." He snapped the book shut, stood, and left the room.

Beauty stared after him. Had she said something wrong? Why would that question bother him so much? Had he lost someone in the war, like the rest of them? Or was he just as fed up with it as the entire Vault?

He didn't return the next night, or the night after, and the pleasure Beauty had gotten from the library diminished. If only her curiosity would do the same. But it didn't. And though she would later tell herself that what happened next was purely an accident, her stomach twisted just a little, the way it did whenever she said something that wasn't quite true.

She was on her way back to her room one night, her nose stuck in the book. She usually tried not to take books to bed because she'd spent more than one night reading until Cybel came to get her in the morning, and she'd blundered through the day in a state of exhaustion, making mistakes and getting scolded by the small bot. But tonight, she just couldn't help herself. She was only four chapters from the end, and if she just—

Where the hell was she? She must've taken a wrong turn somewhere; the corridor she stood in was unfamiliar. *I don't think I've ever been down here before.* Portraits lined the hallway, pictures from another life. Young men and women's faces smiled at her, grinning with the immortality of youth and the confidence of heroes. Some wore civilian clothes, but many more were dressed in the deep green military fatigues of the national army. Official portraits.

I can't remember seeing any of this before. In her mind, she retraced her steps. *I walked down the first hall, turned left, then...*

This must be the Beast's wing. The one place he'd told her never to go. She should turn around right now and get back to her room as quickly as she could, before he or Cybel saw her. She'd managed to avoid his legendary temper thus far, but she doubted he would forgive her after being so explicit that she was never, ever to come this way. But why? What was the big deal about a bunch of portraits?

She couldn't help herself. Slowly, she made her way down the hall, studying each of the images. One in particular drew her eye, and she leaned closer, peering at the individual faces in the group. Her breath caught in her throat.

There he was. Her prince.

He stood at the back of the troop, smiling up at her like he did in the locket, his arm slung over the shoulders of the young man next to him. Like the others, he wore casual fatigues, his face ruddy with health and high spirits. His hair was unruly, not yet cut in the severe style of soldiers, and his skin was unmarked, his clothes freshly pressed.

Her prince had been a soldier. If so, he must be dead. Or at least, his family must be. Why else would his locket be here, among all the things scavenged from those who no longer needed them. Grief and pity for him welled in Beauty's heart and she again made a promise to him. *I'll remember you. And if you're still alive after the war is over, I'll find you and return this to you.*

She traced her fingers over the engraving as she continued down the hall, her trespass forgotten as she tried to memorize all the faces on the wall. Some of them may have died for her, but she would never forget them. *And tomorrow, I'll work even harder to give you what you need to win this war and go on living.*

The hallway ended with a single door. A wildness took hold of her. If this *was* the Beast's wing, the door in front of her must be *his* door. Was he inside? Should she knock? And then when he came to the door, apologize for getting lost and ask him about the portraits? Or should she bust in, demand answers?

Turn around. Turn around, right now.

Then a strangled cry cut through the air from behind the door. Was that him? Was he in trouble? There was a loud crash and the sound of glass shattering. All sinister thoughts of him fled, leaving only the memory of the quiet man reading next to her.

He needs help.

She pushed at the door, and to her surprise, it was unlocked. The assailant must've broken in. Well, she would surprise him.

You don't have a weapon.

She didn't care. She had to help him.

"Stop!" She burst through the doorway, searching frantically for anything she could use as a weapon. On a small table next to the door was an ornate pewter lamp, sculpted into the shape of a slender woman, her arms thrown behind her arched back, like she was soaring toward freedom or death. Beauty grasped the woman around the ankles and swung her up over her head to knock the intruder unconscious.

Except there was no one in the room but the Beast. He stood before her wearing nothing but a pair of loose linen trousers. The floor around him was littered with glass, and a few feet away lay the frame of what had been a mirror.

"Beauty."

The Beast, his chest heaving, his wild eyes fixed on her. The lamp clattered to the floor, forgotten, as she took in the man they feared throughout The Vault.

But he couldn't be called a man. He was more machine than living thing. His face was human enough, it was true, even with the odd light that shone through his irises. His nose, his full lips, and the uncut ivory hair that brushed against his chin, were all undoubtedly human, as was his left arm, well corded with muscle and marred by scars...but the *rest* of him. Skeins of metal fibers and fine mesh formed his cheeks and neck, his collarbone, chest and abdomen, so fine and delicately sculpted they could've been flesh but for the light dancing off the metallic surface. His right arm and hand were also completely machine, but of a much cruder make than his torso, the fingers complexly jointed and archaic. One bare foot was visible under the lined hem of his pant leg, but the other was an even cruder version of his hand, the toes barely anything more than jointed steel.

A cyborg. Inhuman.

Vomit rose in her throat. He was hideous, a true monster. How could he be alive? There seemed too little of his human body left to even be called a cyborg.

"Beauty." He said her name again, and a chill raced up her spine. His voice was low and deadly, like the hum of the vipers that haunted the deep ruins of The Vault before they struck.

She stared at him, too stunned even to scream. She no longer felt her body, only the coldness of his voice mingling with her fear and dissolving her piece by piece.

"Get out."

She met his eyes and was blinded by the fierce life she saw there. He was a miracle. A grotesque, terrible miracle.

"*Get out!*"

His mouth opened inhumanly wide, and his roar wasn't that of one man, but a multitude, discordant and full of rage.

Beauty could no longer endure the sight of him and his anger. She turned and ran blindly down the corridor, taking each turn as it came until she found herself at the main exit. She braced her hands on it, gasping for breath as her heart threw itself against her ribcage, begging for escape. Her mind tried to make sense of the past minutes. Had it truly been him? How could so little of a man be left and still survive? How could anyone human bear it? And yet, the sound that had come from him had been so full of grief and suffering there was no question in her mind that the real beast was whatever monster had done that to him. She'd seen the death of a man and his resurrection as a demon, and suddenly, she couldn't stay there anymore. She had to get out, get as far away from him as she could.

His voice echoed through the corridor, tearing at her heart once more.

I can't leave. I'm trapped here. She pounded on the reinforced door, as though that would make a difference.

"Let me out. I can't stay here. I can't. Not with him."

The door swung open, and Beauty stared at her hands in shock. The corridor to freedom stretched out before her, long and empty, and suddenly, she wasn't so sure.

What do I do? I can't go home.

Not after what Raphael had done. But how could she stay here with the Beast, now that she'd seen his true face, his rage? What would he do to her, now that she knew what he was? And the way she'd reacted to him? No. She had to leave now, while she had a chance. She could worry about the where later.

Just run.

She sprinted down the hallway as though the Beast himself was after her.

Don't look back. Don't look back.

She darted through tunnel after tunnel until, finally, she had to stop to catch her breath. As blood pounded in her ears, blocking out any other sound, she leaned on the wall for support and tried to take stock of her surroundings. Where was she? Nothing around her was familiar.

I'm lost.

Cold fear gripped her. The warren of tunnels under the city could go on for miles. What if she never found her way out? What if she—As she pushed herself away from the wall, her ankle turned under her and she went down hard. Searing pain shot up her leg and a scream tore from her mouth before she could bite it back. She clamped one hand over her lips and the other on her throbbing ankle. *It's okay. It was only one scream, just—*

What was that?

She held her breath, willing her heart to quiet. Was someone there in the dark with her? Her stomach twisted. Was it him? Or something even worse?

"Hello? Who's there?" Her voice echoed back at her in the narrow tunnel. Something shifted behind her, and terror rose in her throat.

Something is here. Something—

75

The dim safety light went out, plunging the tunnel and Beauty into inky blackness. She pressed herself against the wall as flat as she could and inched forward.

Quiet. So quiet. If you can't see them, maybe they can't see you.

But something was coming, something big. Beauty had heard of creatures living deep under the city, remnants from the uncivilized past before Wakelight had been sanitized. But she'd dismissed them as nothing more than a colorful warning to scare children.

Something scraped the corridor wall, something without softness or pity. Rasping breath growled in her ears. It would find her. She reached for the locket hanging over her heart and wrapped her fingers around it.

I'm sorry. I promised I would find you.

But maybe she still would. If he was dead, maybe they would find each other in the light of the afterlife, their reward for losing their lives in the dark.

It stalked toward her. Was it a single creature? On two legs? Or four? Its footsteps came from all directions, eclipsing even her own shallow breaths.

Run.

But she couldn't. As she backed away, her foot slipped on some loose stones, and she fell again. She reached out to save herself, but on the way down, her head connected with the side of the wall.

Numbness spread over her, and the darkness grew soft and deep. Just before she lost consciousness, a roar echoed through the tunnel. Was it the Beast? Had he come for her?

No, not the Beast, but something else fierce and feral, its eyes glittering in the dark and a deep rumble in its chest.

SEVEN

She ran as though the devil himself were on her heels.

Follow her, do something.

But he couldn't. It was only the sharp sting of glass cutting into his foot that finally roused him, and he slid to the floor, his back against his bed.

So she'd finally seen the real him. The Beast. And she'd reacted as he'd known she would. The way they always did.

Almost.

The horror in her eyes had been plain enough, but there was something else there as well. Empathy? Curiosity?

You're just imagining it. What she saw disgusted her. You only want to think she's different.

And why wouldn't she be disgusted? Wasn't that the last thing he'd felt, before he'd brought the mirror down around himself. He'd told Cybel more than once that he didn't want that damned mirror anywhere near his room. But she insisted it would help him accept what they'd done to him, that he had to remember who he was.

Like I could ever forget. Like I don't feel it every minute of every day.

Cybel had been researching radical therapies and believed that if he only looked at himself long enough, he would forgive, would come to terms with what had happened to him and be able to move forward.

I'm letting a robot tell me how to control my feelings.

He shook his head. Should he go after Beauty? Try to explain? Tell her the truth? He crossed one leg over the other and grasped at the shard of glass protruding from the soft arch of his foot. He hissed as he pulled it free, and the blood that flowed out of the puncture released something in him as well. It had been such a long time since he'd seen his own blood.

What little was left of it.

If only I could forget the look on her face.

He'd been instructed to cover himself from head to toe any time he was in The Vault. His kind was forbidden there and would immediately give the truth away; only the need to have someone familiar with the city had made his presence worth the risk. The gamble had paid off. The mask had quickly cemented his reputation, finishing what the violence had started. It had created fear and silence, a much more valuable weapon than anything he'd carried as a soldier.

But not against her. He didn't want her to be afraid of him. *Why? What were you hoping for? You were going to send her home in a few more days anyway, weren't you?*

Of course he was. Still...recently, her company had been almost pleasant. The days had passed quickly in anticipation of their evening ritual. Sitting beside her was the only human contact he'd enjoyed for years. And he'd enjoyed it too much. When she'd asked him about the war, the temptation to tell her the truth had been almost overwhelming. It would've been easy, to look into her eyes and tell her everything that weighed so heavily on his soul.

But it was too dangerous. *She* was too dangerous. She'd stirred something in him, something defiant that had long lurked beneath his skin, that ran through the twisted filaments of his spine.

He'd avoided her the next night, and the night after that, for fear he would feel it again, that the dam would break and everything he held back would be unleashed.

You don't have to worry about that now, not after what she saw.

His heart ached. The last few days he'd felt...what? Not normal, no, but...like a person. The way she'd looked at him in the library as he'd teased her about her romance novel—she'd seen him as a man, not as the Beast. When was the last time anyone had looked at him like that? And what if there *had* been something under her terror? What if it wasn't wishful thinking, and she was what he hoped? What if she *could* understand?

I need to talk to her.

He would tell her everything. His story. Her story. Their past and present.

If he could just get her to listen, maybe she could show him the future.

But to get her to listen, he first had to find her, and apologize. Not for what he was, but for how he'd acted. It wasn't her fault he saw a monster every time he looked in a mirror.

He sprinted from the room and down the hallway, ignoring the shards under his feet. He had to tell her now, while he still had his nerve. Where was she? She had a terrible sense of direction, Cybel had told him. He checked the library, but it was empty, as was her bedroom. Where the hell else could she be? She couldn't have—

"Are you looking for Beauty?" Cybel stood in the doorway of the control room.

"Have you seen her?"

"Yes."

"Where is she?"

"Gone."

"Gone? Gone where? How could she get out?"

"I let her out." The robot's bland expression infuriated him, even if it was the only one she had.

"You *what*? Why would you do that?"

"She's not a prisoner here. Is she?"

"No, of course not, but—"

"She was pounding on the door, terrified. And you were screaming and— I've never heard you scream like that. I thought—"

"You thought I might *hurt* her?"

Cybel said nothing.

"How could you think that?"

"You've become unpredictable. You are no longer yourself."

It was true. But— "I would never hurt her, Cybel. No more than I would hurt you. I—"

"Well, I didn't know that." The little bot huffed. "I like her. I didn't want—"

"I like her too." He pushed his hand through his hair and swore. "We have to find her. It's not safe out there. She doesn't know where she is."

"And you can rescue her. A knight in shining armor." She gave a little spin.

What? Surely she didn't— He glared down at Cybel. "You didn't really think I'd hurt her, did you?"

"No," she admitted.

"Then what the hell are you playing at? She could be in danger." He strode to the front door.

"Cillian! Your hood." She sped after him, clutching it in her hands.

"I don't need the damn hood. She's already seen me." He took a deep breath. "Cybel, if something happens to her—" He let the warning hang over the robot's head.

Cybel was undaunted. "Nothing will happen. She might be scared, but then you'll come swooping in to save her. Like in her romance books."

"Those books usually end up with one or more of the heroes dead, Cybel."

"Oh. I didn't read all the way to the end."

Cillian closed his eyes and prayed for patience. "Is that what you planned? To put her in danger so I could save her? What were you thinking?"

"That you're a good man. And that she's the kind of person who'll be able to see that. She just needs a little push. This is the perfect opportunity." Was that smugness in her tinny voice?

But maybe...

"I've got another plan. I want to tell her...everything."

Cybel rotated on her jointed waist the way she did when she was agitated. "Are you sure that's a good idea?"

"I don't know. But I won't find out until I talk to her. I just need to find her." He opened the door then turned back to Cybel. "If she comes back, please, keep her here. Whatever it takes."

"I w—"

A faint scream echoed through the air.

Beauty.

EIGHT

Beauty's tongue lay thick in her mouth, and her temples pounded with an unceasing ferocity. What had happened? The last thing she remembered was eyes in the dark, the glowing eyes of a savage beast. Then...nothing.

She struggled to sit up. As her eyes adjusted, she made out the shape of walls, of a bed. *Her* bed.

This is my room. But how did I...

The Beast. It must've been him she'd seen in the dark. He'd come after her and brought her back. She scrabbled backward, pressing herself into the corner at the head of her bed. What was going to happen to her now? She'd seen his real face, had run from it. Panic climbed the walls of her ribcage, sinking its sharp little claws into her and making it hard to breathe.

Would he kill her? She bit her lip to suppress the whimper threatening to escape. She never should've gone down that hallway. Never should've opened that door. But she had, and now she truly was a prisoner, locked away until he decided what to do to her.

No. I refuse to cower before him. If he's going to kill me, he can get it over with. I'm not going to sit here, caged like a sheep waiting for the slaughter. How could he do this to her? *You're an idiot. You thought that because he like books, he's somehow less of a beast?* No. That was what he truly was. She'd just been stupid enough to forget. And where was Cybel? *She fooled you too.*

She climbed off the bed and stood on shaking legs. She would pound on the button beside the door until it shorted out. She would throw herself against the door itself, bruising her fists on the cold, uncaring surface until the Beast came. Then she would look him in the eye and show him that even if she was terrified of him, he wasn't going to break her. He could kill her, but he wasn't going to—

The door slid open.

It's not locked. I'm not a prisoner.

She retreated to her bed, letting the door glide softly back into place. What was going on? Had he simply come after her and brought her back? But why, after what had happened? Why would he— Had he just wanted to make sure she was safe? He wasn't angry with her?

Relief warred with a creeping remorse. Even after the way she'd acted, he'd come to find her, still wanted her under his roof. And she'd immediately assumed the worst of him. She gazed at him again now, in her mind's eye. She'd never forget what she'd seen. His ruined body, intentionally inhuman. The anguish and anger as he'd seen her. She'd run from him then, but now her memory couldn't turn away.

Had she been wrong about him? What would've happened if she'd reacted differently when she'd seen him, stood her ground?

But I had to run.

Why? Because of the way he looked?

No, it was because he screamed at me. I thought he was going to attack me.

But had she really? If he hadn't looked so frightening, would she have felt the same way?

Think back. Did it really seem like he was going to attack you? Or did his body make everything you feared about him seem true?

She forced herself to relive their confrontation. The Beast, his devastated body. The broken mirror. Something terrible had happened to him. Something worse than she could ever have imagined, and she'd blamed him for it.

And she'd been trespassing, catching him in a vulnerable moment. No wonder he'd been upset. He had to know what she'd thought of him. Creatures like him...cyborgs were an atrocity, an offense against the human soul. At least, that was what she'd always been taught by the stories of a world beyond Wakelight, beyond Heartcrown.

Everything must've been right there on my face. It was cruel, really, what I did to him. He had a right to be angry.

She was a fool.

He obviously wasn't proud of the way he looked, didn't want the fear his appearance provoked. Why else cover himself up? Yes, the mask was scary, but not as horrific as the truth.

His real face. I wish I could remember what it looked like. But all I saw was a monster.

What if she'd made a huge mistake? What if he wasn't the monster everyone thought he was? He'd obviously been loved once, and had loved, if the portraits he'd kept were anything to go by. And not once had he shown her anything but respect. He'd been invisible a lot of the time, and brusque when he was there, but...

He gave you a room, food...and a library.

Was it possible she'd run away from something good, just because it was ugly?

He's not ugly. The vehemence of the thought surprised her, even more so because she meant it.

The truth was painfully clear. The monster was her.

For the next hour, her mind ran in circles. What was she supposed to do now? How could she face him? He'd brought her back, so he didn't want her to leave...but now that she knew the truth, what *did* he want?

Her eyes eventually grew heavy and she curled up under her covers. As she waited for sleep to claim her, she comforted herself with thoughts of her prince.

What would he do in my situation? A prince would never run away.

She brought her hand up, reaching for the familiar shape of the locket.

The locket.

It was gone. Had she dropped it? She leaped out of bed and scrabbled about the floor, nails scratching the tiles as she searched every inch of her room. She squinted in the gloom under the bed, trying to catch its golden glint. But it was gone. Had it fallen off? Or had *he* taken it from her?

Somehow, that was worse than everything else that had happened, its loss cutting deeper than her misery and confusion.

Finally exhausted, she fell asleep, her hand clutched to her chest where the locket had lain, over the heart that threatened to break.

* * *

When she woke, a tray had been placed on the table in the corner of her room. How long had she been asleep? She must've slept deeply not to have heard the tray being brought in.

But she was awake now, and she had a plan. She was going to find the Beast and...well, that part she hadn't *quite* figured out. But she would know what to say when she saw him. She hoped.

She devoured the bread on the tray, gulped down some water, then quickly changed into something not covered in dust and grime from the tunnels. Her hand trembled as she ran a brush through her hair. Already her nerve was beginning to slip.

You can do this. If he can live through...whatever happened to him, can live the way he is every day, then you can at least look him in the eye.

Straightening her shoulders, she went to the one place she hoped he would be.

He was sitting in his high-backed chair when she came into the library, facing away from to her. All she could see of him was his hands, gripping the flared arms.

She took a deep breath. "Bea—" *I don't even know his name.*

"I was thirteen years old when the war began. How old were you?" His voice held a softness, a dreamy, faraway quality she hadn't heard before.

He wanted to talk about the war? She lowered herself gently into her chair, trying not to break his thrall. "Nine." Old enough to remember the chaos. The smoke, the fire, the screams. The silence.

"Do you remember much of your life before?" He stared off into a distant corner of the bookcase. His mask was back on, his hood pulled up over his head.

"A bit, but not much. It's more of a feeling than actual memories, you know? Everything was so clean, and sterile, and bright… Ordered, I guess."

"What about your parents, your family?"

Beauty did remember them, no matter how hard she tried not to. "Yes. They died on Day Zero. They were teachers, and the school… I was home sick that day." They'd been in a rush to get to work that morning, late because her mother didn't want to leave her. Day Zero had been the first day of the war for Wakelight. "You?"

"My parents worked in defense."

"They built The Vault?" The only thing that had saved Wakelight from obliteration. Even so, there had been rioting the day it rose, too late to stop the first wave of attacks. "I remember the riot."

"Yes." Bitterness laced his voice. "People didn't understand how hard they'd worked to try to get it finished in time. They knew trouble was coming, months before it happened, but it still wasn't enough time. They took the blame, even though they saved hundreds of thousands of lives." His fingers tightened, sinking into the fabric.

"I'm sorry." What must it have been like for him, to see his parents frog-marched in front of a baying crowd?

"I became a soldier when I was fifteen." His voice was even softer now.

"Fifteen? I didn't think they took anyone that young."

"They didn't. Not at first. But two years into the war, we were outnumbered, outgunned. The enemy had technology that we… That we couldn't match.

We were losing." He shook his head and gave an acrid laugh that burned the back of Beauty's throat.

"So they began accepting whoever they could recruit. Of course, for those of us whose families were dead, it was an easy choice. The only choice we had, really. Not all of us were taken in by strangers, so where else could we go? We underwent training for six months then they shipped us out."

"To the front line?"

"Yes. We were barely more than weapon fodder at that point, although I was luckier than most. I was tall and strong for my age, so I was able to handle more powerful weapons, like the older men. And so we fought, losing more ground each day."

"But then how did you end up here? Surely they still need every soldier they can get?"

He didn't seem to hear her. "A few days after I turned seventeen, my unit was caught by surprise."

Beauty thought of all the portraits running along the Beast's corridor. Had the same thing happened to them? Were any of them still alive?

When he didn't continue, she prompted him. "But you survived."

His laugh this time was brittle. "Barely. I was one of three, and the only one still alive." He took a deep breath. "Most of my body was destroyed."

It hung between them. *Most of my body was destroyed.* Beauty's heart picked up in a painful rhythm.

"The only way they could save me was to make me a cyborg. Some days, I don't know why they bothered. There was so little of me left."

Cybel. *He's sacrificed more than most.*

For Wakelight. For her. "I'm so—"

"There's so much I want to tell you, but if I do—" He exhaled heavily. "You can't leave here. You could never go home."

"Okay."

"Okay, what?"

"Tell me, and I'll stay."

"Beauty—"

"I am home. I want to stay." It was a surprise even to her. But something had shifted inside her, waking from a stupor to raise its face to the sun.

There was silence from the other chair. Could he hear her heart pounding in her chest?

"Hello?"

"Are you sure? Even knowing what I am?"

"I don't care about that. I never should've run away. I just— What I saw... I admit, it was a shock. But I— It doesn't matter."

"It doesn't?" The hope in that one question was almost more than she could bear. How had she ever thought him a monster?

"No. And I'm so sorry. I—"

He held up a hand. "Beauty... The other things I need to tell you...there is so much more to my story—and yours."

"My story?"

"Yes. But it will change everything. If you don't want that, you need to leave here and never come back. I know it's selfish. But you're the only person who knows the truth about me, and I can't live with half-truths any longer."

"Why me?"

"Honestly? I don't know. I...feel like you would understand."

"I can't make you any promises, but whatever you have to tell me, I'll at least listen."

"That's all I ask." He shifted in his chair and turned to her, his eyes glittering behind the mask.

The mask. He didn't need to wear it anymore, not in front of her. She didn't *want* him to.

"But first, take off the mask."

His hands stayed where they were, his fingers curling into the chair arms once more.

She persisted. "Please. Take off your mask."

When he didn't move, she stood, leaned over, and raised her hands to his face. He held his breath as she pulled off his hood. His pale hair fell forward and she smoothed it back. He tolerated her touch until she brushed the edge of the mask.

"Beauty." He wrapped his fingers around her wrist. She let him lower her hand. "Are you sure about this?"

"Yes."

He took a deep breath and pressed the side of his temples, and after a soft click, the mask came away. The Beast dropped to the floor with a clatter, and the man sat before her, his eyes wary.

Beauty couldn't help herself. All she saw now was him. She traced her fingers over the side of his face, across the seam where man and metal came together. He closed his eyes. "Does it hurt?"

"No." His eyes flashed as he opened them, lit from within by a pale silver light.

The eyes in the darkness. For an abomination, they were beautiful. "What's your real name?"

"Cillian."

It suited him.

"I'm so glad you're still here." Cybel rolled into the room and Beauty stepped away from him, suddenly self-conscious. "I told him it was a lot to take in, that telling you everything was a terrible idea, but he was right about you."

Beauty looked sharply at Cillian. "What does *that* mean?"

"Well, it's a big deal finding out the world you live in is a lie, right? I'm glad, though. It's been a terrible burden for Cillian to bear, and now—"

"I haven't told her *everything* yet, Cybel." He pressed his lips together.

"Oooh. I—"

"What does she mean, Cillian? What lie?" Whatever it was, it must be big. And bad. *The world you live in is a lie.*

He sighed. "This is part of what I wanted to tell you."

"Tell me now." It had to be about the war. Nothing was more important than that.

"I— I think you should rest first, Beauty. It can wait. I—"

"I've rested enough." *In fact, I feel like I've been asleep my entire life.* "What about the war? Are we losing?" *The Vault will fall. And we'll be overrun. We'll—*

He shook his head once then crossed his arms over his chest. "That's just it, Beauty. There is no war. Not anymore. The war ended five years ago."

NINE

She swooned, staggering a little.

"Beauty!" He lunged forward, catching her before she fell. Her eyes were closed. He shook her gently, but there was no response. Had she fainted? If she had, he wouldn't be surprised. That was a perfectly fair reaction to finding out the cause you'd been devoting yourself to for most of your life didn't exist.

I should've prepared her more.

Or maybe telling her anything had been a mistake. But it was too late now; he couldn't take it back.

"Sorry, Cillian."

"It's okay, Cybel. She probably would've had the same reaction no matter what."

All they could do now was wait. He took a moment to study her. She looked so vulnerable and peaceful with her blanket tucked up under her arms, he didn't want to rouse her. Soon enough, she would be awake, and then she would remember.

But until then, he allowed himself to hope. She'd stayed. *Wanted* to stay. His relief was almost painful. She'd chosen to stay with him. And more than that...

She wanted to see my face. She didn't flinch. She...touched me.

No one in The Vault had ever seen his true face before, let alone touched him. He'd waited so long for that day to come, and yet, it was bittersweet.

There's no going back now. What if it's all too much? What if this has been a huge mistake?

What if she wasn't who he thought she was?

A long lock of brown hair curled over her shoulder. His hands ached to touch it, a different hurt than the ghost-pain that normally haunted him, but no less intense. It had been years since he'd touched another person that way.

Don't forget yourself, Cillian. She might not still think of you as a monster, but that's only a start. Don't prove her wrong now by acting like one.

His face still tingled where she'd touched him, and he closed his eyes again, savoring the moment. He would always remember the look on her face as she'd run her fingers through his hair, over his skin. She had seen *him*. And she hadn't winced or looked away.

She stirred, her forehead creasing as she opened her eyes. For a moment, she seemed confused then her eyes widened, and she sat upright, pushing the blanket to the floor. What if she'd changed her mind about staying? Was there anything he could say to change it back?

No. Let her get her bearings and remember on her own.

But impatience got the better of him. He'd waited for this moment too long. "Beauty, I—"

Her head whipped around. "Where—" Her voice faded as her mind worked through the last few hours. Emotions crossed her face one after the other—confusion, fear, then a horror that made him want to stop time and fold her into his arms, holding her until the world passed into something new and painless.

She remembered.

"It can't be true."

"Which part?" He held his breath.

"The war. I— It can't be."

"Why not?" *Let her work up to it.*

"Because then everything... I—" The struggle on her face was so clear. Would she faint again?

He reached out to put his hand on her arm, to comfort her, then snatched it back. If she rejected him now, at this fragile beginning... "Let me tell you the whole story then you can decide. Please?"

She nodded, but the look she gave him now was cautious, calculating.

She's trying to work out if I'm a madman. The Beast. Just be grateful she's not screaming the roof down. But she was still looking at him without disgust, without fear of *him.* For now, that would have to be enough. He just had to tell her the truth. After that...

He leaned back in his chair, trying to look nonthreatening. "The war lasted for four years altogether. And it only went on that long because we kept trying to negotiate, to find a peaceful resolution. But neither side would give even an inch to the other. So we kept fighting."

"I'm not surprised. Why would we ever think the invaders would negotiate with us?"

"The day I was...injured was the last day of the war. We were making our final assault with everything we had. We knew we couldn't win. By this time, the enemy had decimated our ranks. We had one desperate chance. And we lost."

"We lost the war?" Her voice was small.

"Yes, Beauty. We lost. We fought so hard, but in the end, it wasn't enough. We were overpowered."

"But then why haven't they invaded The Vault? How is it still standing?"

"There was no invasion. The enemy was our own." He waited for it to sink in.

"Our own... I don't understand."

"Heartcrown forbade androids and human augmentation a long time ago. But not everyone agreed."

"But there was a vote—"

"Yes. But was it legitimate? Who knows?" He flexed his metal hand. "Many didn't think so. They wanted Heartcrown to progress, like the rest of the Republic. When they spoke out, they were...suppressed."

"We didn't hear anything about that."

He arched an eyebrow at her. "It was before we were born. As far as we knew, it was unanimous. But history is easily rewritten."

"How—"

"They hid in Heartcrown, building their army with help from others in the Republic."

She shook her head. "Didn't the rest of the country notice when they...attacked us?"

"Blackmoth was in turmoil then. There was very nearly a civil war. Armies were being built all over the place." And yet, only rumors had reached the depths of Heartcrown.

"The entire Blackmoth Republic was at war?"

"Nearly, but a disaster stopped it before it could start." He shrugged. "Then, when The Vault went up, it shrouded Wakelight from the outside world. The rebels took advantage of that."

"And now?"

"And now, we're part of a province called Foxwept. But *we're* still hidden." He ran his hand through his hair. "Us and all the other domed cities in Heartcrown. The rest of Foxwept don't even know we exist." And if Grace Alpha, the rebels' new capital, had their way, no one ever would.

"Our own people fought against us?" Her face was pale, her lips bloodless.

"They weren't *our* people. We persecuted them. We forced them to become their own people."

She frowned. "You sound...sympathetic."

"I wouldn't be alive if it wasn't for the 'enemy.' Who do you think made me a cyborg?"

"Why did they save you?"

"Well, it wasn't from kindness, if that's what you're wondering. Our numbers were depleted, but so were theirs. They kept all survivors alive in any way they could."

"That must've been terrible for you."

"It was. On one hand, they destroyed everything I cared about. On the other, they allowed me to live. Selfish, right? I'm so damn grateful to be alive, even...like this."

"It's not selfish." Her voice was soft. "So how...how did they finally win?"

"The plague."

"You mean the sleeping sickness? The one that killed almost everyone in The Vault?"

Thousands of people had gone to sleep one night and never woke up. For weeks, their bodies had lingered, alive, unable to wake, until they'd eventually starved to death.

"Yes. It was created in a lab as a biological weapon. They knew they would eventually win, but the toll was getting too high. They needed victory to be easier, faster. So they took drastic action."

"But it didn't kill all of us."

"Some people were immune. They considered it a kind of selection process for the future."

She looked like she was going to throw up. Should he stop now? It was a lot to take in. When he'd first found out, it had almost been too much. He'd almost...

But you didn't. And this is no longer about you.

Whatever she was feeling, she pushed it down. "Then what?"

"Then it was over. The survivors started to rebuild only a few miles from here. They created a superior AI, Grace Alpha, and named their new capital after it. They updated laws, began a fresh era of civilization, one that embraced transhumanism and humanoid artificial intelligence."

"But what about us, in The Vault? And the other cities? I don't understand. If the war is over, even if our side lost...why are we still here? We're just civilians. The war had nothing to do with us." Her brow creased again as she searched for an answer. "Or is Wakelight keeping them out? But then why do we... I don't understand."

This was the worst part. The part he woke up to every day, the knowledge choking him like poison. "Wakelight isn't keeping them out, Beauty. It's keeping you in."

"But how could Wakelight let that happen? It's supposed to protect us."

Her naïveté was like shrapnel to his heart. "Wakelight is the one who suggested it."

"I—"

"Wakelight's just a branch of the Grace Alpha AI. After the war ended, the citizens of Grace Alpha asked it what the best plan for the future would be. It advised them to start again. Integration, infrastructure, rebuilding— It would be incredibly time consuming and expensive. In the end, the people of Grace Alpha kept the future to themselves."

"So outside this city, there is no war?" She chewed on her lip. "But the burning we can smell, the sounds of bombing?"

"All a construct of The Vault."

"And the promises they made to us? About when the war is over?"

Cillian looked at his hands. "They make all kinds of promises."

"And everything we scavenge, grow, build?" Her questions were coming faster, the edge in her voice sharpening.

"The capital city uses it to supply itself. All the food goes to their tables. The fabrics, their clothes…"

"And the artifacts we risk our lives for?"

"Knick-knacks for their fancy houses."

"But the people in City Hall, how much do they know? Have they all been lying to us this entire time?"

"There's nobody in City Hall, Beauty. Just Wakelight. Nobody's been there for years."

"Wakelight abandoned us." Her voice was dull.

Had she finally understood? Finally accepted? Could it be that easy to convince her?

It wasn't. She shook her head. "No. That's too… That's just not possible. We can smell the land burning some days. We get updates on the progress of the war. We—" Her gaze fixed on him. "What about *you*? You've been here for as long as I can remember. The timeline doesn't add up."

He shook his head. "The mask. I'm not the first Collector for this district. My predecessor was also a cyborg. It's our way of paying for our survival."

"How long have you been back in The Vault?"

"Four years. Give or take." When the Collector before him had died, Cillian had been sent back home. They'd asked him to betray his own— And he'd done it.

"I'm sorry, but I just can't believe you." She rose slowly from her chair, keeping her eyes fixed on him, wary. "Am I a prisoner here?"

"No, of course not. I told you that before. I gave you the option to leave."

"What if I said I wanted to leave now?"

His heart plummeted. He didn't want her to go. Not now, when he'd finally found someone to share his burden with, someone who'd seen his real face. "You can go. But Beauty—"

"Even if I said I was going to tell everyone what you've just told me?"

Was she testing him? Threatening him? "Do you think they would believe you?" He raised an eyebrow. "Or do you think they would hang you for heresy? Do you think the laws here are made by The Vault's own citizens?"

Or by others, encouraging fanaticism to do their dirty work for them?

The color drained from her face. She knew the answer as well as he did.

Be gentle. She still might stay. "Could you really go back, Beauty? Knowing what you now know?" he asked as calmly as possible, when all he wanted to do was grab her by the shoulders and shake her.

101

If she left here, they might— And it would be his fault. He never should've brought her here.

She hesitated. Did she believe him? Or was she just stalling for time, thinking of the best means to escape?

She stopped edging away from him and lifted her chin. "Show me."

Show me.

"Show you?" Wasn't his body evidence enough?

"Until I see it with my own eyes, I can't believe you." She squared her shoulders and glared at him.

"I've told you everything. I—"

"I've been told things my whole life," she pointed out. "And now you're *telling* me they're not true. Until I can actually *see* the truth for myself, I can't believe anything." Her hands gripped the back of the chair. She wasn't as poised as she pretended.

"I know you think I'm telling you a story, or that this is some kind of sadistic game. But it's not." He flexed his cyborg hand. "I don't know how else to prove it to you."

She changed tack. "Why are you telling me these things? Me specifically?"

"Because you're not like the others. You... I don't know exactly. You just seem different. Look, I'm taking a huge risk here. You could go running to Quinn, or someone, anyone, and tell them the things I've said to you. It would get back to the capital and they would come for me, for both of us. So ask yourself, why would I tell you these things if they weren't true? If I didn't think you would believe me?"

"Maybe you're crazy."

He shrugged. "Or maybe I'm telling you the truth."

She kept up her interrogation. "Why do they trust you, Cillian? Why have they put you here? Are they not worried that you, or any of the other Collectors, will tell the truth?"

"No. We've been promised a place in the capital when our jobs here are done." He gave a harsh laugh. "I've even been promised a new body."

"So why are you risking it by telling me?"

"Because I don't believe them. They bought my loyalty with this body. But I heard their promises five years ago, and they haven't kept a single one. I'm tired of their lies, of what they've done to our people."

"I am too."

"So you believe me?"

"I didn't say that. But I am willing to entertain the idea that you might be telling the truth."

He breathed a sigh of relief. She'd probably seen the cracks in The Vault's facade herself, whether she was consciously aware of it or not. He'd often wondered if there were those who suspected their lives might not be what they seemed.

"But I need proof."

Proof? "I—" How? How could he prove it? There was very little evidence in The Vault. And what there was could easily be explained away.

Even as he pushed it away, an idea began to form. It was dangerous, and incredibly risky...but it would give her the proof she needed, and they might not get a chance like this again. "I think I know how I can show you."

This is mad, Cillian. You could get both of you killed.

103

"Why do you suddenly look like that?" She broke his reverie, deciding him.

"Like what?"

"All intense, like you're about to go back into battle?"

"Because I am. Beauty, have you ever been to a ball?"

TEN

The plan was crazy. Every single bit of it.

You believe him, don't you? So why are you making him do this? But Beauty had to *know*. She paced back and forth in the library, wringing her glove-clad hands together.

Sit down. Just sit down and take a breath. She began lowering herself into her chair.

"Don't sit down!" Cybel barreled into the room. "Stop!"

She leaped back onto her feet, heart pounding. "Why not?"

"You'll wrinkle your dress."

"Does it matter?"

"Of course it matters! You have to fit in. Do you really think the young ladies of the capital go to balls in wrinkled dresses?"

"I wouldn't know, would I?" Beauty replied tartly. "I've never even worn a dress."

"It is beautiful, though, don't you think?" The little robot gave an almost-human sigh.

It *was* beautiful. The women in the capital clearly lived a much different life than hers.

The gown was a rich golden-yellow, a full silk skirt overlaid with fine layers of floating chiffon. The heavily jeweled bodice was held up by two ornate straps that curved over her shoulder blades, leaving her back bare.

She didn't know whether to love it for its beauty or hate it for what it represented. *Can I do both?*

"Go on, give us a twirl," Cybel urged her. "Just one. I want to make sure it's right."

"Is that *really* why?" What was she going to do if it wasn't right? Did she have a whole closet full of these dresses?

"No. I just thought it might be pretty." She peered up at Beauty, the lenses of her eyes glowing. "It's not like *I* get to go to the ball, you know."

"Is that a guilt trip?"

Cybel said nothing. *But if she had lips, I bet they'd be quivering right now.*

"Fine. But I feel ridiculous." She spun on her toes, the skirts lifting and flaring out to twirl around her.

"Well, I think you look...stunning." Cillian stood in the doorway, unmasked and ungloved, his eyes wide as he took her in.

Beauty flattened the skirts with her hands. "Cybel made me." Could he see the heat in her cheeks?

Cillian laughed. "Don't worry, I had to do a spin for her as well." Though he smiled, he stood stiffly, looking as uncomfortable as she felt. He wore a suit of deep midnight blue, cut expertly to his frame. It hid what his body was made of, but not its shape, hugging his broad shoulders and solid arms. His hair was freshly cut at the sides, the long hair on top combed back. He looked alert, his eyes sharp and watchful. As she gazed at him, the light in his eyes shone.

You're staring at him.

He took a step toward her. "Beauty—"

The warmth in her face deepened, spreading throughout her body. By the time he stood in front of her, she was on the point of bursting into flame. She tilted her face up to his and as he gazed down at her, the flicker of light in his eyes turned into a glittering inferno.

I wonder if this is what the stars look like. It had been years since she'd seen them.

He raised his hands to her shoulders. *Is he going to kiss me?* Panic flashed through her. She'd never kissed anyone before. Had never cared to. Did she want *him* to? He was *the Beast*, for goodness' sake. And yet, she didn't move. Didn't even want to.

His lips parted as he lifted the hair at the back of her neck, and she took a deep breath.

"Here. I thought you might want to wear this." He withdrew his hands and she looked down. The locket.

"Where did you find it?"

"You were wearing it when I found you in the tunnels. I— I took it back."

"I'm sorry. Cybel didn't think you would miss it. And I just—" *What? Opened it and fell in love with the man inside?* "I thought it was beautiful," she finished lamely.

He smiled. "I'm happy for you to have it. If you want it, that is."

"I do...thank you." *Just ask him.* "Cillian?"

"Mm?" He was gazing at the locket, his face unreadable.

"Who is the young man in the picture? Do you know?"

His expression was wistful. "It's me. It was taken the day before my injury."

It's him. Cillian is my prince. He always has been. Her pulse quickened, and yet a tiny part of her soul cried out that it had known all along, even if she hadn't. "You look so...much older than seventeen."

"We all looked older. I'd been in the war for two years at that point. Nothing ages you faster than thinking every day might be your last."

"But your hair—"

"Turned white after I got blown up. The doctor said it was the trauma. It happened overnight and never went back."

"Who was the locket for?" She bit the inside of her cheek. Did he have a girlfriend? Had he got it made specially, only for her to die? The locket burned against her skin, rebuking her.

"My mother. I— I'd planned to put it on her grave one day. I know it seems silly, but—"

"It doesn't." She put her hand on his arm. "Why didn't you?"

"I don't know where she's buried." He turned away. "Just another one of their lies."

"I'm so sorry." The loss of her own parents was something Beauty would never forget. They'd died in the first wave... and she'd been alone. They hadn't been given a proper funeral either.

He took her hands in his. "Are you sure you want to do this? These people are dangerous. They believe in a better future, it's true, but they will see it succeed at all costs." His fingers gripped hers gently, the metal of his cyborg hand smooth against her rough skin. "Beauty?"

She took a deep breath. "I'm sure." *I need to see it for myself.*

His hands tightened on hers. "Listen to me closely then." He squeezed her hand until she raised her eyes to his. "We have to do this properly. If we get caught...if *you* get caught, I—" He didn't finish, but his meaning was all too clear. *I won't be able to save you.*

"Tell me." She squeezed his hands back, stroking the smooth metal before she could stop herself. It was just so different from human skin. If he noticed, he didn't react.

He called out over his shoulder. "Cybel? Do you have the masks?"

"Masks?"

He grinned. "Didn't I tell you? The ball tonight is a masquerade."

"Masquerade?" She'd read about masques, and despite his warning, despite the fear she would've been sensible to feel, a thrill of excitement shot through her. Never in her life had she been to such a thing, had never even heard about one outside her books. They had parties in The Vault, of course, but she usually avoided them. They tended to be strange affairs, somber at first, devolving rapidly into drunken brawls and clandestine hookups. Fierce, frantic, and bloody. Kaitlin had loved them, but Beauty would've much rather had a page of paper between her and all that revelry.

"Here, Cillian." Cybel rolled up to them. Was that a hint of resentment in her tone?

"Can...can robots not come?" Maybe Cillian would let her, if he was going to bring Beauty anyway. They could keep each other company. Cybel's eyes flashed with hope, her head swiveling up toward Cillian.

He frowned. "No. I'm sorry, Cybel. But you know—"

"Know what?" Offense on Cybel's behalf rankled Beauty. "I thought they liked robots."

"They do. Just not *my* kind." Cybel spun and rolled from the room, the masks dropping from her small fingers as she fled.

"I— I'm sorry. I didn't mean to upset her."

"You didn't." Cillian sighed as he bent to retrieve the masks. "She's right."

"What did she mean?"

"They like androids—humanoid robots. Robots like Cybel are seen as obsolete, as a slightly embarrassing reminder of how primitive they used to be."

"Like me."

He gave her a half-smile. "Yes, like you. Hence why you need to be so careful." He held up the smaller of the masks, an intricate golden filigree. "You must wear this at all times. Do not take it off, no matter what. You never know if they have spies in The Vault who may recognize you." He held onto it as she tried to take it from him. "I mean it, Beauty. If they realize you're not of Grace Alpha, and even worse, from The Vault... No matter what they say, no matter how beautiful they tell you you are..." The words hung between them for a few moments, until Cillian cleared his throat. "You must keep it on. Do you understand?"

"I understand." She pried the mask from his hand and turned it over in her fingers, anything to distract herself from the compelling glow in his eyes. The mask would cover only the upper half of her face, a network of intricates curves and curlicues so interwoven that, although it gave the impression of being delicate, would conceal her identity, leaving only her mouth and eyes exposed. Above the crown stretched a pair of ears of the same swirling pattern, tall and pointed. "A rabbit."

His smile held no humor. "Yes."

"And you?"

He held his up with a raised eyebrow. His was much heavier, solid metal covered with tiny, painstakingly etched hairs. A wolf. How apt.

"So now what?"

"Now we go. But remember—talk little. Observe a lot. And don't let me out of your sight. I promise to keep you in mine." He led her from the room, from the safety of her new...*home* and into the shadowy tunnels below. As the darkness swallowed them, she pressed the locket to her heart.

I'll keep you in mine.

ELEVEN

I never should've agreed to this.

As they sped farther and farther away from The Vault, Cillian's unease grew like a cancer, eating away at him, until it was all he could do not to engage the brakes and send them hurtling back the other way. He would bundle Beauty into his arms and carry her into the library, throw her into her chair, and pile enough books around her that she wouldn't be able to read them all in an eternity. They would sit there together until the end of time, everything outside his walls a ghost howling into the wind, ignored and powerless.

Instead, here they were, tearing toward...what? The truth? Yes, but then what? Once she knew the truth, what would she do? He'd lit the fuse without really understanding the bomb on the other end.

And yet, he was electrified, every nerve in what remained of his body on fire. Finally, someone other than him would know the truth, would understand. Right now, that was enough, the giddiness of a shared secret. For how long, he didn't know, but it didn't matter. For the first time in years, someone had seen him, Cillian. Not the monster he was in The Vault. Not a toy, like he was to those in Grace Alpha. He hated these parties, the long looks, the unbidden and unwelcome hands touching him, inviting and sinister. The fact that his body was so heavily augmented, yet still human in all the ways that counted, made these events a dance of diplomacy and refusal that he tried to avoid at all costs.

And yet, it would be worth it if Beauty believed him. And so they raced through the dark under the earth toward a world Beauty had never seen.

What would she think? How would she see the night sky full of stars? The air, fresh and clean and free of plague, or filth, or sorrow? The people dining on plates she may have risked her life to procure? The laughter of those whose only care was for their own comfort ringing in her ears?

He glanced over at her. She was composed, looking out the small window into the darkness, eyes downcast from her reflection. He would find out soon enough. He was going to stop the shuttle about a mile from their destination. It pained him to let her go for even a minute, but if someone saw them arriving together, it would attract unwelcome attention. He would go first, with her following behind. That way, he could watch her the moment she arrived.

If something happens to her, you'll never forgive yourself.

His eyes were drawn to the locket around her neck. When he'd seen it on her as he'd carried her back from the tunnels, his first instinct had been to snatch it from her, to hurl it into the darkness, to bury the Cillian who would never exist again. How could he compete with that memory? But he hadn't been able to. Instead, he'd unclasped it and slipped it into his pocket. He'd quizzed Cybel about it later, and she'd admitted she'd left it out for Beauty to find, although she refused to tell him why.

"You can't take that away from her," the little bot had admonished him.

"Why not? It's mine. You think I need her comparing what I am now to the man I used to be?"

"You're still that man, Cillian."

"Well, she's not going to see it that way, is she?"

"You don't know that."

But he did. And yet, when Cybel had been about to leave the room, she'd turned and looked up at him, the light of her eyes an innocent blue. "She holds it when she goes to sleep at night." Then she'd rolled away, damn her.

Was it true? And did it even matter? He *wasn't* that man anymore. Certainly not in Beauty's eyes. Still, he'd carried the locket with him over the next days, something he'd never done before. And then, when he'd seen her all dressed up, so delicate she could've passed for any young woman in Grace Alpha, yet with a core of steel none of them would ever have, it was as though his hand had moved of its own accord, pulling the necklace from his pocket and clasping it around her neck. And she hadn't flinched, despite how close he'd been to her. So close he could smell the floral rinse Cybel had given her for her hair. So close, that if he'd tilted his head just the right way…

All too soon, he brought the shuttle to a stop. The station had been abandoned years ago, and hopefully, the overgrown and derelict building would keep their arrival hidden. The door slid open, and the cool night air enveloped him. He breathed deeply, steeling himself.

Her hand touching his face, not with the curious lust for an oddity, but with wonder.

Whatever happened tonight, he would have that to hold onto until the day he died.

Hopefully, that wouldn't be tonight.

"Do you smell that? What is that?" Beauty had appeared at his elbow, her pale face raised to the sky as she gulped in breaths of fresh air. She stepped gingerly, her eyes darting back and forth, as though expecting to see the evidence of a war she didn't yet believe was over.

Well, if this doesn't convince her, I don't know what will.

The Vault, although ventilated, probably hadn't had truly clean air in years. "That's what real air smells like." Maybe it would be enough, and they wouldn't have to go to the ball.

She turned in a slow circle, her eyes closed. "It smells like...like... I can't even describe it." Then she opened her eyes and let out a shriek.

Cillian's heart leaped into his throat as he lunged toward her. "What? What is it? Is someone here?" There shouldn't have been anyone this far out, not with the wilderness taking over. But there were creatures other than humans that lurked in the dark.

Her face was turned to the sky, her fingers pressed to her mouth.

"Beauty?"

Wordlessly, she pointed up at the dark night.

The sky was clear, scattered with millions of glittering stars holding court for a full, golden moon. His heart squeezed, a stifling mix of joy and sorrow. "How long has it been since you've properly seen the stars?"

She stretched her arms out from her side and spun, the skirts of her gown whirling with her. "I

115

can't even remember. Aren't they wonderful?"
She stopped spinning and grabbed his arm.
"Thank you so much for this." Her expression
turned somber.

"Are you okay?"

"I just can't help but wish…that the others
could see this. The others in The Vault." She
frowned. "Do you think they'll ever get to?"

How could he answer that? With the truth? Or
his suspicions? He chose truth. "I don't know."

She nodded, but the excitement had gone from
her face. She looked pale and drawn and
vulnerable, and again the desire struck him to
push her back into the shuttle and leave. It would
be so easy to let shining stars and sweet air be her
memory of the night.

Too easy. This sweetness would be more lethal
than the hornet's nest he was about to take her
into. This was all beauty, all good. She needed to
see the ugliness in order to truly understand what
was at stake.

"Are you ready? We can still—"

She straightened and smoothed her skirts. "I'm
ready."

* * *

He kept glancing over his shoulder as they
made their way to the manor in which the ball
was being held. At least it wasn't within the city
walls. That would've made it a lot harder to get
Beauty in. She moved like a ghost through the
countryside, a specter swathed in gold. He had to
keep waiting for her to catch up, so easily
distracted was she by even the smallest flower
illuminated by shafts of moonlight.

And he...he was *smiling*. That was almost as surreal as what they were about to do. *Are you sure you're not dreaming?* For a long time after his injury, he'd lingered in a gauzy dream state, warm and peaceful. When he'd finally awoken, it had taken him a long time to adjust to living again in the real world. Now, with Beauty floating over the grass, raising her hand in reassurance every time she spotted him, he could almost believe he was back there, straddling the line between life and death.

He shook himself. *Get your head on straight. We're almost there. You need your wits about you.* The grass changed abruptly from weeds and wildflowers to the expertly manicured lawn of the manor. As he stepped onto the paved driveway, the great house loomed in front of him, a triumph of wealth and architecture. No one knew how old it really was. Not that it mattered to Grace Alpha. They'd gutted much of the inside, covering the timeworn stone with materials more suited to their modern tastes. Materials taken from the hands of those in The Vault. A tribute to their devotion they would never get to see.

He glanced back. Beauty was standing still, her eyes fixed on the manor. Was she going to back out now? Well, if she turned around, he would too.

But she didn't. She stepped onto the drive and raised her hand to the locket. Catching his eye, she nodded once.

That's your cue.

He approached the front door, the hair standing up on the back of his neck as it always did. Couples were walking through the open double-doors in front of him, and beyond them, the main floor of the manor appeared to be packed. It looked like almost everyone in Grace Alpha was there. Good. The more people, the easier it would be for them to blend in.

And for you to lose each other.

The man on the door inclined his head at Cillian. He'd been a soldier as well, though not of Cillian's squad. But like him, he bore the marks. Under his mask, a long scar bisected his face, one side man, the other machine.

"Cillian."

"James. Good to see you."

"I'm *surprised* to see you. You don't normally entertain these things." There was no suspicion in his voice, just curiosity.

"I know. But I was given a hint that maybe I should make an appearance." He shook the other man's hand. "You know how it is."

"Don't I just. Well, it's going to be a busy one tonight. If you find yourself at a loose end, feel free to join me out here. I know you can't stand the crowds."

"I may just take you up on that." Gold flashed in the corner of his eye; Beauty had nearly caught up. "Well, I'd better go be seen." He gave James a companionable smirk then stepped over the threshold. Almost immediately, he was swallowed by the crowd. Now to find somewhere he could keep an eye on Beauty. He scanned the room, searching for the best vantage point. There. On the stairs.

He'd just taken up his post when Beauty came through the door, followed by a low bow from James. Was it just him, or was there a slight hush when she entered? No heads perceptibly turned, but...how could they not notice her? She moved with a grace that far exceeded the other young women there. Years of scavenging in the most unlikely places had given her an agility that these pampered socialites would never possess. Although her head was held high, her eyes were cast demurely down, just as he'd instructed her.

It must've taken every ounce of her self-control. If she'd thought the night sky was opulent, what must she think of this house and the people in it? He wished everyone was gone but her. He could imagine her running from room to room, her exclamations of delight. But she would understand soon enough the rot this golden veneer covered. Indeed, she was already beginning to, if the tremors in her hands were anything to go by. Surely she'd seen enough to convince her he'd been telling the truth?

"Cillian. What an unexpected surprise."

Damn. He didn't have to turn to know the speaker. "Aren't all surprises unexpected?"

The man laughed. Gideon Black. Cillian's handler and a basic bastard.

"How are you doing? It's been a while." His onyx mask boasted a long, curved beak and gold-rimmed eyes. A cuckoo. A parasite.

"It's been busy." Cillian gestured to the crowd. "We've had a lot of requests."

"Well, you won't have to worry about that too much longer."

Cillian turned, trying to keep his expression neutral. Inside, his heart doubled its rhythm, and phantom pain tingled in his fingertips. "Oh?"

"Resources are getting scarce, as you know. I doubt we'll be able to squeeze The Vault much longer. How long do you think? Until it's stripped bare, that is?"

Gideon knew the answer as well as Cillian, so why ask? Cillian sighed. "About a month. With the exception of agriculture, of course."

"Yes, that's what I figured as well." He tugged on the bow at his neck, pulling it straight. "What a shame. It was great while it lasted." He bared his teeth at Cillian. "Oh, well. That'll still give us enough time for the GA-85126 to be ready for deployment." Androids were to take up the labor needed to support Grace Alpha, now that the sentient androids in the rest of Foxwept had been emancipated. They would continue to build and to serve.

"What will happen to The Vault? When it's over?"

Gideon narrowed his eyes. "Does it matter?"

Do thousands of lives matter? "Just curious. I do live there, after all."

"Not for much longer. Once The Vault is finished, your role there will be too."

My usefulness, you mean.

"And then The Vault will be collapsed."

"Collapsed? What about the people inside?" He couldn't possibly mean—

"There are always casualties in war, Cillian, as you well know. This war needs to be finished cleanly, no loose ends."

"Loose ends? Those are people, Gideon. People who've lived their lives on their knees so you can stand on their backs. They've been promised a future in return, a life." At worst, Cillian had thought those in The Vault would be abandoned, the people released into the outside world despite Grace Alpha's promises to give them a home—a fate that had already sickened him. But at least then they would've had a chance to build something for themselves, even if they had to scrape and claw their way from the bottom to get it. This...this was cold-blooded murder of the very people who'd made Grace Alpha possible.

Gideon laughed. "Why so melodramatic, Cillian? Where could they possibly fit in with Grace Alpha? With Foxwept Province? They were against us, remember? All this devotion you're talking about wasn't to us, it was to our enemy. They'll get what they deserve. Nothing more, nothing less."

Cillian's mouth went dry. It was all he could do not to drive his metal fist into Gideon's sneering face. How could the man be so merciless, so cruel? Those people, people like Beauty... The image of Beauty's body—covered by a layer of gray ash, lying twisted and broken in the rubble of their home—flashed through his mind. Would she call out for him? Or would she curse him?

It doesn't matter. Because that's not going to happen. Not to her.

The seams where his flesh met metal burned, mocking him and the deal he'd made with the devil before him. Over the roaring in his ears, he barely made out more of Gideon's lies.

"...and anyway, you don't have to worry. You'll get what's coming to you, as we discussed. A home in Grace Alpha, eh? Won't that be nice. Retirement, at your age? I wish I was so lucky. And hey, you can settle down. It's not like you're short of admirers." He nudged Cillian in the ribs and nodded toward the grand foyer.

More than one woman stared up at them, raking over his body with hungry eyes. And at the back, near the wall, Beauty. She gazed up at him as well, the expression in her eyes unreadable. As one of the women noticed Cillian's attention had shifted from

Gideon, she made her move, slinking up the elaborately carved staircase to where the men stood and running her hand over his cyborg arm with a lascivious slowness before standing on her tiptoes to whisper in his ear. Whatever entreaty she made, he didn't hear.

Beauty was gone.

TWELVE

Beauty was nearly blinded as she crossed the threshold. Never in her life had she beheld such color, such *shininess*. Everything gleamed—the walls, the floor, the ceiling, the people...even the food seemed covered with a glossy sheen. It was so different from the muted browns and grays and grime of The Vault that her eyes couldn't make sense of it. A soon as she was able, she retreated to the wall, pressing her back against it for comfort.

The longer she looked, the more her eyes adjusted, and at last, she was able to truly *see* what was before her. She'd never seen anything so grand. It was just like the castles in her books, the vast room decorated almost entirely in gilt. She'd hadn't known so many shades of gold existed. It covered everything, from the soaring, arched ceiling to the silver-veined marble floor. Even the walls were a textured gold that seemed to shift before her eyes. Had Cybel known when she'd chosen Beauty's dress, hoping it would help her blend in? If so, it worked. Hardly anyone seemed to notice her, and she took the opportunity to stare.

Just off the main foyer was a large doorway leading to a ballroom, where couples dipped and spun, their masks and clothing a swirling, glittering myriad of rich color painful to look at. It didn't seem real. She'd expected to see people at a party, of course, but the amount of wealth, the sheer flaunting of it was staggering.

In the corner where she stood was a large painting of a young woman reclining on a chaise, her face pale and wan but for two rosy spots on her cheeks. She was dressed all in white frills, and her hand was raised to her forehead as though she'd been caught in a swoon. Beauty knew the painting well. She'd recovered it months ago. In fact, if she looked closely enough, she could still make out the specks of blood on the underside of the frame where Red had touched it after slicing herself on a shard of exposed metal. She'd caught a fever from the wound and almost died.

Beauty hadn't doubted Cillian, not really, but the painting was a fist to her stomach. All that time she'd truly believed that the rarities they'd been risking their safety for had been sold to other countries in exchange for aid, or broken down, or sent to the front as symbols of inspiration to the forces there. But no, here they were, just another luxury among millions, a momentary pleasure soon forgotten. Everything Cillian had said was true.

Cillian. Where was he? She'd promised to keep him in her sight. Beauty pushed herself away from the wall, her eyes scanning the cavernous room. There. On the staircase speaking with a man in a bird mask. Whatever they were talking about, Cillian didn't look happy. His face was creased into a frown, his shoulders stiff. And yet, in his suit, with his silver hair falling over his eyes, and his cyborg hand gripping the rail, he was striking. His physical presence dwarfed the man next to him even though they were of a similar height. He seemed different here, among these people. He stood straighter, his head higher.

Despite what he's accused them of, he can be himself here among them.

The Beast. But he wasn't. That title belonged to the architect of The Vault. Was that person at the party? Was it the man standing next to Cillian? The air seemed to go out of the room then, and Beauty blinked, trying to push down the panic rising inside her.

Cillian. I need to speak to Cillian.

But how? She couldn't go up to him. Could she signal him, somehow? She stared at him, willing him to look her way.

And he did.

But as their eyes met, a woman in a beaded violet gown slid around him, caressing him, up his arm, over his shoulder. She smiled into his face, pressing her lips to his ear. What was she saying? She certainly didn't seem to consider him a monster. Just the opposite. Her hand left his arm and slid lower, and—

Beauty couldn't watch anymore. Something burned behind her eyes, something new and fierce. She wanted to push through the crowd, grab the woman by the hair, and snarl at her, like a feral animal.

Get your hands off him. He's— What? Mine? I barely know him. And I certainly don't know him in this world.

She had to do something or she was going to scream. When had she gotten things so confused?

I have to get out of here.

But she couldn't. She might not be able to find her way back to the shuttle. And then what? There didn't seem to be any fighting going on, but who knew what else lurked out there?

Her gaze was caught by the buffet table and she made a beeline for it. If Cillian could tear himself away from that woman, he could find her there. If not...well, at least she could keep herself busy until it was time to leave.

The table practically groaned under the weight of the food on it. Meat, cheese, exotic fruits...and pastries. So many pastries. *How do I even remember what one is?* But the thought was drowned out the moment she bit into one, the crust flaking between her teeth. *Heaven.* But then The Vault crept into mind and the tart turned bitter in her mouth. She tried to swallow and nearly choked.

"Here, drink this." A statuesque woman masked as a horned horse handed her a slim glass flute of something sparkly.

Unable to speak, Beauty accepted the glass and poured the contents down her throat, gasping as the effervescent alcohol burned all the way down.

"Better? Lura's tarts can be a bit dry. Problem with her program, I think." She gave Beauty a crooked grin.

"Thank you." Beauty tried to cover her mouth as she coughed at the lingering sting. What must this woman think of her? Cillian had said to blend in, and here she was, choking on the tarts.

"It's a lovely party, isn't it?" her savior asked. Her gaze was oddly intense, and Beauty got the feeling the question wasn't a simple one.

She straightened, brushing off a crumb that had fallen onto the neckline of her dress. "Yes. It's very...luxurious."

The woman's scrutiny didn't ease. "That's a diplomatic way to put it." She stepped over to Beauty and leaned in close. "Disgusting would be a better word, don't you think?" Her gaze traveled over Beauty, lingering on the locket.

Was it a trick? What could Beauty possibly say? Of course, she agreed, but...this woman was one of *them*. What if she said the wrong thing? All she could do was stare back, like the rats she sometimes stumbled over in dark corners, their eyes wide in the beam of her light. She stalled for time, clearing her throat. "I—"

"Don't be deceived by what you see with your eyes." The woman glanced up to peer over Beauty's shoulder. "Though something tells me that perhaps you aren't."

What does she mean—

"Excuse me? Could I have this dance?"

She turned. The man who'd been speaking to Cillian stood behind her, bowing from the waist as he offered her his arm. She took it gratefully; anything to get away from the other woman's knowing look. But before she could step away, the woman hugged her, pressing her cheek against Beauty's. "Watch out for that one," she whispered. Then she was gone.

The man led her through the swirling crowd to the middle of the dance floor then clasped one of her hands in his and wrapped the other around her waist, drawing her close. Too close.

"I don't think I've met you before, little rabbit." The hooked beak of his mask curved over her shoulder, prodding her closer to him.

What did she do now? There was something about the man that made her skin crawl, something *wrong*. Cillian had told her to stay as inconspicuous as possible, and she'd blown it. But what could she have done? He didn't seem like a man easily refused.

Stall. You'll think of something.

"Oh?" She kept her voice low, modest. Hopefully he would mistake it for shyness.

"I thought I knew every young lady in Grace Alpha. And yet, here you are." His hand tightened on hers; he expected a reply.

She had to say something. *Cillian, where are you?* But she didn't dare look for him. This man was like a viper, a creature you didn't take your eyes off, no matter how much your mind screamed to run the other way. Do that, and he would attack.

"I normally prefer reading to dancing."

That seemed to amuse him. He threw back his head and laughed, too loudly. He pulled her even closer and smiled down at her, prompting the couples closest to them to grin knowingly as he bent to whisper in her ear.

"Are you sure? Does this not please you?" He closed what little space remained between them, the length of his body pressing against hers. The hair on the back of her neck prickled with an unpleasant heat, and she tried to lean away from him, but he held her so tightly it was as though her body was welded to his. A bead of sweat trickled down her back.

He spoke again, all playfulness gone. "Who are you?"

"I—"

"May I cut in?" Cillian appeared at the man's elbow. The light in his eyes flared as his gaze passed over them.

"Must you, Cillian? I haven't met this young lady before, and I have to say, I find her very intriguing." His smile was friendly, his tone anything but.

Cillian's returning smile was brittle. "I'm afraid I must. If I don't, I suspect Serena will eat me alive." His gaze flicked to the purple-gowned woman who'd been so eager to see him earlier. She hovered now on the edge of the crowd, her eyes pinned to him.

"Ugh, that woman." Beauty's partner shook his head. "Not one for a subtle chase." For a moment, it seemed as though he would still refuse then he loosened his grip and leaned back to look down at her. "I'm sorry our time's been cut short, little rabbit." He raised her hand to his lips. "Perhaps we will meet again, in more...secluded circumstances." As he stalked away, he said something to Cillian too low for Beauty to hear. Which was probably for the best, given Cillian's dark expression.

As the other man was swallowed by the crowd, Cillian picked up Beauty's hand and slid his own arm around her waist. She opened her mouth to speak and he shook his head. "Not yet." He moved them in unison with the other dancers, twirling Beauty through the throng until they came to the edge of the dance floor—the opposite side from the now-glaring Serena—where they still blended with the crowd yet had a modicum of privacy.

"I thought we couldn't be seen together." She kept her voice as quiet as possible, barely moving her lips.

"I know, but watching Gideon come on to you like that...that was a path I couldn't let you go down." His grip tightened as he spoke.

"Who is he?"

"The man I answer to." Loathing lurked under his calm tone.

129

"He seems…"

Cillian's grip tightened further, and a muscle twitched in his jaw. What was going on with him? "Yes?"

"Creepy, to be honest."

His hand loosened, albeit only a fraction. "That he is."

"And her? That woman who was…talking to you? On the stairs? Who is she?" She forced herself to be nonchalant. Her eyes focused on his left shoulder, where a strand of hair had fallen.

"Serena? She's…"

"A beautiful woman. And she seems to like you—" What was she saying? Heat crept up her neck and into her face. *Hopefully he'll think it's just from the dancing.*

His arm around her waist stiffened, his metal fingertips pressing into the small of her back. Had she said something wrong?

"She's not beautiful to me. And she likes anything damaged."

Indignation stiffened her own arms. "Cillian, you're not—" She stopped as his hand tightened on hers again. Why was he so agitated? His movements were irregular, almost clumsy, and his grip was becoming painful.

"Are you okay? You're…you're going to break my fingers."

He stopped and looked at their entwined hands, her reddened fingertips. Chastened, he loosened his hold. "Beauty, I'm sorry. I—"

"Come on." She tugged his hand, pulling him away from the dance floor and behind one of the great pillars that lined the room. All along the wall were small, cushioned alcoves, thankfully empty. Maybe here they could speak properly without being overheard.

"What's going on with you?"

"I just... This was a stupid risk, Beauty. We never should've come here."

Was that why he was so upset? It wasn't going that badly, was it? At least now she knew the truth, had seen it with her own eyes. That was what they'd come here to do, after all.

"But it's fine, Cillian. I believe everything you told me now. I—"

"It's not fine. It's far from fine." He bit off each word, and his inhuman irises blazed—not the pale light she'd seen in the darkness but the shrinking of his pupils, a warning.

Was he angry with her? "Cillian, I'm sorry. I—"

"We have to get out of here, now."

Already? True, only moments before, she couldn't wait to leave. But now they were together, and there was still so much to see. Surely they could stay just a little longer, watching from the shadows? She might never get another chance to see a life so exotically different from her own. "But—"

"Do not forget where you are." The edge of his voice was diamond-sharp, slicing through the seductive miasma of the ball.

He was right. What the hell was she thinking? These people were perfectly happy to keep her and her kin in squalor, working their nails down to the quick so they could while away their lives at parties like this. There was more food on that table than the Hallow Hands saw in a month. She peered around the pillar.

She could see it now, so clearly, the decay underneath the shiny veneer. How easy it was to forget, to admire them. And the worst part was that if anyone from The Vault saw what she was seeing, they would only redouble their efforts, determined to one day make it into this heaven. They wouldn't even care about the lies, the lost years. They would get down on their knees and thank these monsters for their salvation.

She pulled back and looked up at him. His face was pale under his mask, and something wild fretted in his eyes. What might it cost him to have brought her here? She was suddenly aware of how great a risk he'd taken, just so she would believe him. He didn't have to bring her here, risk everything for her if they were caught. But it had been so important to him that she believe, and she'd insisted that this was the only way. He had much more to lose than she did, and still he had put himself in danger. For her.

Beauty stood on her tiptoes and cupped Cillian's face between her hands.

"Beauty—"

She pulled his face down to hers and kissed him. His mouth opened in surprise, and she took the opportunity to deepen the kiss. He sighed against her mouth with a shudder then wrapped his arms around her, his human hand tangling in her hair.

She traced her fingers over the seam on his face as he shifted her around and pushed her back to the pillar. She arched her back against the cool stone, pressing against the unyielding plates of his mesh chest until she could feel his heart beating over hers. Could he feel it? Their hearts, beating together? As though in answer, his mouth hardened on hers, became more insistent. His metal fingers slid up her spine, coaxing a small moan from her throat. Her first kiss, with him. With—

He pulled back abruptly, and she staggered in the sudden void between them. "Cillian?"

He turned away from her. "We have to go. We can't—"

What was wrong? Did he regret what had just happened? Mortification shortened her breath. He'd seemed like he'd wanted it as much as she did. Maybe she'd misread him. Her head spun. She shouldn't have drunk that glass of...whatever it was. Here they were, supposed to be keeping their wits about them, and she'd kissed him. What was wrong with her? "Cillian—"

"Now."

Bowing her head so he couldn't see her shame, she began walking back toward the dance floor.

"Not that way." He grabbed her hand, and she tried to ignore the heat that crackled up her arm at his touch. "Down here."

He led them swiftly through a series of corridors. How many times had he been here, to know his way around such a maze? But then, it wasn't that different from home.

Just more traps to fall into.

At last, they came to a much smaller door. A smaller, *locked* door. Cillian swore.

"Can you open it?" If not, they were going to be trapped here.

"Yes, but not without leaving a trace." He sighed. "Well, there's nothing to be done about it. We can't stay here." He pressed his hand to the panel on the wall and a moment later, the door slid open to reveal a set of stairs and the night sky. He stepped out first and scanned the vast lawn. "Come on, let's go."

The door had led them to a side exit of the manor, out of sight of the main entrance. Light spilled onto the front lawn, and laughter carried over to them, but they kept to the cover of the sculpted ornamental bushes, darting from shadow to shadow like a pair of apparitions. Finally, they reached the line where the manicured lawn again became wilderness, and Cillian allowed her to slow to a walk.

She pulled her hand from his and bent over, trying to catching her breath. A stitch protested in her side, and she held up a hand as he looked questioningly down at her.

"I'm okay. I just need a minute."

He nodded, though his expression was anything but happy. He kept glancing back toward the manor, as though he expected someone to come after them. But no one had seen, she was sure of it. "Okay, let's go."

The ride home was tense. Pain still lanced her side, and Cillian kept his face turned away from her, studiously staring out the window into the darkness. Should she apologize for kissing him? Would that make things even more awkward? His hand rested on his lap. What would he do if she touched it? Would he pull away? He'd held her hand while they were running, but that was different. That was for survival. This was for...what?

In the end, confusion kept her hands where they were. What had been in that drink? Her head was muddled, her body in a state of chaos. Her lips still tingled from his, her fingertips remembered the silkiness of the hair at the nape of his neck. She pressed her forehead to the cold glass on her side and closed her eyes.

Just think about something, anything else.
But she couldn't.

THIRTEEN

Cillian closed his eyes against his reflection as they barreled through the dark. His heart beat so painfully, so loudly, it seemed to fill the small shuttle. In just a few short hours, his world had been turned upside down again, by both Gideon and the young woman beside him.

Gideon was going to kill everyone in The Vault.

And Beauty had kissed him.

He couldn't decide which was worse.

What the hell was he supposed to do now? That single kiss had changed things, had changed *him,* a sweet, intoxicating poison. The only thing he knew for certain now was that no matter what else, he wasn't leaving Beauty to the fate of The Vault.

A month, Gideon had said. One month until the end. *It'll probably be the only promise he ever keeps.* Cillian was under no impression that Gideon would keep his promise to him. *A home. Retirement.* A lie. He would be retired all right— to his death.

That wasn't going to happen. They could leave, tonight. He would take Cybel and Beauty somewhere hidden, somewhere safe. Where that would be, he had no idea, but it wasn't important. Right now, getting them out was all that mattered. Anything could happen to him between now and then. When he'd spoken to Gideon, there'd been something in the other man's demeanor, as though Cillian was already under suspicion. But how was that even possible?

You're just being paranoid. Besides, you haven't done anything yet.

Except ask questions. And people like him had disappeared for less.

It had to be tonight. Tomorrow at the latest.

Decided, he leaned against the window, staring into the gloom.

She'd taken his face in her hands, as though it were a normal face. And she'd kissed him like...like it was a normal kiss, a moment of genuine passion. Spontaneous. Because of *him*. Before when he'd been kissed by women, they'd done so with only their own pleasure in mind, for the thrill of making love to a man who was mostly a machine. He had all the exotic spice of an android but a mind of his own, which made it a challenge. Cillian was a rare prize indeed. Others like him enjoyed the attention, but he never had.

But someone like Beauty...it was more than he'd ever hoped for. When he'd been cyberized, he'd given up the expectation of a normal relationship, of an equal love.

Who said that's what she's offering you?

It must've been a heady night for her in so many ways. Now that they were back in the shadows, did she regret the moment of impulse? The softness of her lips, the desire in her hands as she'd pulled him down to her. Giddiness wanted him to touch his hand to his lips, to feel the invisible mark she'd left there.

He hadn't wanted to pull away. If he could have, he'd have stayed in that moment forever. It might be the only moment they ever had, given their fate. After the initial surprise, the flush of pleasure, all he could see was The Vault, caving in and entombing the people within its protection. Entombing *her*. What would she say when she found out what Grace Alpha had planned? Would she blame him?

He'd find out soon. The shuttle came to a smooth stop, and the door slid open to reveal Cybel, waiting, her face blank. At the sound of Cillian's boots on the platform, her eyes blazed into life. She must've been waiting there the whole time. Affection rushed through him. Another to keep safe at all costs. She was the most loyal friend he'd ever had.

And the nosiest.

"Well? How did it go?" She made a whirring noise, her equivalent of an excited squeal. All her resentment at being left behind seemed forgotten.

"It was...interesting." He turned away from her to help Beauty off the shuttle. She was perfectly capable of getting off herself, but he didn't trust that damn dress, stunning though it might be.

You just want an excuse to touch her.

She didn't look at him, although she did accept the hand he offered her. "Thank you." Her voice was barely more than a whisper, and as soon as her feet touched the ground, she was off, hurrying away from them without a backward glance.

What was going on with her? He'd thought she'd come back home to Cybel and he'd have to spend the next few hours listening to them go over every tiny detail from the party.

Cybel waited until she'd turned the corner before rounding on Cillian. "What did you do?"

"Me? Nothing! Why do you think I did anything?" Although she was only three feet tall, the small bot had a way of making him feel like a child. *Her* child.

"Well, *something* happened. Was it the party? Was someone mean to her?" Her ocular interface flashed.

"No. I—" Might as well come clean. She'd find out sooner or later. "She— We kissed."

"You *what?*" There was no mistaking the glee in her tinny tone. "*Cillian!*"

"I— Don't make a big deal out of it, please. I'm not sure if she's happy about it. You saw what happened just now." He dropped his voice as low as he could. "And Cybel, we've got bigger problems."

"Bigger than you finding love? How is that possible?"

"Cybel, I'm not joking. It was a kiss, nothing more."

"*Yet.*"

She was exasperating. "Look, let's go inside. I need you to bring Beauty to the library. Please. I have to talk to both of you."

* * *

Where could he start? How could he possibly tell Beauty that in one month, everyone they knew in The Vault, even The Vault itself, would be gone? What Grace Alpha was already doing was bad enough, but at least there'd still been some kind of hope, hadn't there?

He paced alongside the bookshelves. Where the hell were they? How long did it take to get out of a dress? He'd been too agitated to change his own clothes, conceding only to remove his mask and jacket, and loosen his stiflingly high collar.

Just as he was about to erupt, Beauty and Cybel arrived. *Finally.* "Sit."

She can't even look at me.

It didn't matter. She could regret everything that had happened since they'd met—including the kiss—all she wanted, he still wasn't leaving her to the mercy of Grace Alpha.

He softened his tone. "Please."

Beauty sat, still carefully avoiding his eyes. Cybel remained by her side, her little fingers curled over the arm of her chair.

He cleared his throat. "Something happened tonight. Something that changes everything. Something terrible." Why was he stalling? *Just say it.* "I—"

"I'm sorry!" Beauty was on her feet, her eyes blazing. "I thought...I thought you—"

Cillian blinked. What was she talking about? "Beauty, I'm sorry, I don't—"

"You don't have to apologize." Indeed, her expression suggested that apologizing made it a hundred times worse. Whatever *it* was. "It was my fault, and I understand that you don't want... That I—" She drew a shuddering breath.

Cillian dove in before she could speak again. They didn't have time for this. "Beauty, what the hell are you talking about?"

Now it was her turn to blink. She frowned. "The kiss." When he didn't reply, she rushed on, the words tumbling over each other. "Look, I'm sorry. I shouldn't have kissed you. But I thought...I thought you—" She inhaled deeply. "I thought you wouldn't hate it. And I'm sorry. I won't do it again. Things can go back to the way they were, and—"

"No, they can't." *That* was what she thought this was about? How could she think he'd be anything but thrilled about what had happened between them? It was all he could do not to sweep her off her feet and kiss her again. He would've laughed if he wasn't about to break her heart—just not in the way she expected.

"I'll go then. I can go back—"

He crossed the space between them in three steps. "Beauty, stop."

She bit her lip and looked up at him.

He put his hands on her shoulders. "That's not what this is about, I promise. Why would you even think that?"

"Because you pulled away. I— It's fine, if you don't see me that way." But her expression suggested it was anything but fine.

A wild dizziness nearly overcame him. She thought he'd pulled away because he didn't want her? He almost wished that were true. Even that would be better than the news he had.

"Beauty." He cupped her face in his human hand, running his thumb over her cheekbone. "I didn't pull away because I don't want you." He leaned down and brushed his lips against hers as she stiffened in surprise. "Believe me, I *want* you to kiss me, Beauty, and I want to kiss you back. I can think of few things I've wanted more."

She searched his face, as if she could see the truth there. "Then why?"

"Because I have something else to tell you." He led her gently back to her chair. "Please, sit." As she did, Cybel shifted closer, curling her fingers around Beauty's. They both stared at Cillian, and for a moment, he considered simply not telling them. Why not just whisk them away from here?

Under the guise that you've simply had enough. Then, when it happens, you can plead ignorance. They'll never know that you knew. It won't be you who breaks her heart.

But it just wasn't in him to lie. Not anymore.

"Do you remember the man I was speaking with at the ball? Gideon? The one you danced with. He's told me about the future of The Vault." He ran his hand through his hair. Where should he start? "So we were—"

"Cillian? Why are you talking so much?" Cybel knew him too well.

Just say it. "In one month, The Vault will be destroyed."

For a moment, Beauty didn't speak. Then she smiled. "But isn't that a good thing? Doesn't that mean they're going to announce the war is over?" Her eyes shone as she considered the possibilities. "We'll be able to go outside...start new lives. Why do you look so miserable about that? I mean, people will be angry at first when they find out, but once they see what their new lives will be, they'll—"

"They'll never find out, Beauty." This was worse than he'd thought. It had never occurred to him that she'd misunderstand.

She frowned. "What do you mean?"

"In a month, they'll collapse The Vault in on itself. With everyone inside."

"But they'll die." She said it as though the idea hadn't occurred to him.

And there's nothing we can do to stop it. "Yes. Its usefulness is over. As Gideon put it, Grace Alpha don't want any loose ends. They have the future they wanted."

"But they can't— What will we do?" Her lips trembled, and she pressed them together.

"We'll leave. Tonight." As soon as they were ready.

She was shaking her head. "But how? Where would we go? And how could we get that many people to—"

"I'm not talking about everyone in The Vault, Beauty. I'm talking about us. You, me, and Cybel. I can get us somewhere safe. It won't be easy, but—" *We may just make it.*

Beauty rose from her chair. "Us? Just us? You're going to just let everyone in The Vault die?" She clutched at her throat, as though the dust had already settled in her lungs.

"What other choice do we have? We can't stop Grace Alpha. Escaping tonight is our only chance. You need to start packing."

She took a step back, and Cillian breathed a sigh of relief. He'd been afraid she was going to fight him on it. She was still so loyal to her Guild, despite what Quinn had done to her. But she clearly saw they had no choice. So where should they go first? Straight out of the city? Or move around for a few days then—

"No."

"No, what?" In his mind's eye, they were already fleeing under cover of darkness. The shuttle could be traced, so they couldn't—

"I'm not going." She stood defiant, her feet planted, her arms crossed over her chest.

"What do you mean, you're not going?"

"I *can't* just run away with you tonight."

"Okay, fine. We can go tomorrow. But it has to be—"

"I can't go at all!" She looked incredulous, like the entire idea was ridiculous. "We can't leave everyone in The Vault to die."

"But, Beauty—"

"No! I won't do it."

"We can't evacuate everyone. It's just not possible."

She chewed on her lip. "Fine. But we have to at least tell them. Give them a chance—"

"What chance? We can't tell them. Do you have any idea what would happen?"

She raised her chin. "They would fight for their lives. They would—"

"Panic. They would spend the next month in chaos. Who knows what they'll do to themselves? To each other?" He didn't want to be there to see it.

"But they can *escape*. They can leave The Vault. If enough of us do it—" Her voice rose, the words tumbling over each other.

"They can't leave, Beauty. The Vault isn't meant to keep people out. It's to keep them in. There's no way for them to escape." The memory of burning flesh still made his nose itch.

"There must be."

How could she still believe they had that choice? "Think about it. Other than the Collectors, have you ever heard of anyone leaving? For anything?" As she opened her mouth to reply, he clarified, "I mean actually *leave*. Not just set out to."

She hadn't, of course, because no one had. The charge on The Vault saw to that. Death was instantaneous, the bodies secreted away in the dark. It was the second-best-kept secret of the city.

Her face was pale. "But we have to do something."

"We will. We'll escape, and we'll live." He reached out and took her hands.

The paleness evaporated, replaced by a blazing fury. "You would save yourself and leave them all to die?"

"I'm saving *you*. You and Cybel are the only ones I care about." It was harsh but true. Once they were safe, he'd worry about everyone else.

"Don't you dare put this on me! We have to tell them, Cillian." She stood stiffly, unyielding, as she glared at him.

"We can't. *You* can't. We—"

She yanked her hands from his. An expression had returned to her eyes, the expression he'd dreaded ever seeing again. Her voice shook. "You really are a monster. A selfish, murderous monster."

"Beauty—"

"No." She turned and fled the room.

"Come back!" He sprinted after her. Why couldn't she see this was the only choice? Yes, it was selfish, but he didn't care. All he wanted was to see her safe. Damn the rest of them. She didn't understand what it would be like, to see everyone she knew die around her and know she was next. He did. And even if she hated him for the rest of their lives, at least she would be alive to do it.

He caught up to her at the front door. Her chest rose and fell as she took deep, gulping breaths, and as she heard him behind her, she turned on him, her lips pulled back from her teeth in a snarl. "Get away from me. Don't touch me."

"Stop. I—"

"Let me out."

"No."

"I said let me out!" She pounded her fists on the door. "Let me out!"

There was no way he was opening that door. "What are you going to do? Tell everyone? Do you think they'll believe you?" If she would only just stop and think about it, she would see there was no other option. They couldn't fight this. The best they could do was try to survive.

"I don't care. I have to do something. If I tell them, even if only some of them believe me—"

"And word gets out? And gets back to Grace Alpha? What's to stop them from collapsing The Vault tomorrow? A few vases? Some scrap metal? You mean nothing to them." He reached out for her. "But you mean something to me." *You mean everything.*

She slapped his hand away. "Open this door, *now.*"

"I'm not opening the door. Beauty, listen to me. You—"

The door slid open. They both stared at it in shock. How—

Cybel.

Beauty saw her chance and was through the door before Cillian could react. His reflexes weren't what they used to be. He started after her, but— His mask. He couldn't go anywhere without his mask. If even a single secret got out now, it would open the door for others. "Beauty, stop! We can talk—"

She stopped at the end of the narrow corridor and braced herself against the wall. "I'm done talking to you. Forever."

And then she was gone.

FOURTEEN

She made it around the corner before the tears came. They flowed fast and hot, making it difficult to see where she was going. She took turns as they came, randomly and instinctively, until, finally the warm air and smells of The Vault bathed her face. She staggered to a halt, trying to catch her breath. Would he follow her? She strained to listen but could hear nothing in the tunnels behind her other than the echo of dripping water. She didn't know whether to be relieved or angry.

How could he be so cold? So cruel? After everything that had been done to all of them, how could he think of simply leaving everyone to die? He hadn't even considered an alternative. His only concern had been to get out as soon as he could, to save his own skin.

And yours.

How could he think she'd be all right with that? How could *he* be? Everything she'd ever heard about him was true—he was more machine than man. And yet he'd fooled her, had made her believe he was something different. Someone different. Someone she could...

And I kissed him.

She wiped at her mouth, as though she could erase the last few hours. Well, she'd gotten away from him. And not a moment too soon.

But what was she supposed to do now? She had nowhere to go, not until she'd decided what she was going to do about The Vault.

Her feet turned toward the city square. The night market would still be open; there were a few hours left before sunrise. Maybe some familiar sights and smells would help clear her mind. A couple walking toward her stepped off the sidewalk to give her a wide berth; word must've spread that she was the Beast's now.

If only they knew the Beast wasn't their biggest problem.

She came to the edge of the market square, an outsider looking in. Most of the food stalls were still open, the scent of roasting meats and vegetables thick in the air. The tables in the center were full of people, some coming home from a disappointing night, others just heading out. All talking and laughing, blissfully unaware. It was surreal, every bit as much as the ball. Only now did the horror she should've felt earlier—first when Cillian told her the truth about the war, then later, at the ball—grip her. But that had been too bizarre. Cillian, all of it...it was too much like a dream. Her disbelief had buffered her against the truth at first then—despite the ugly reality just below the glittering surface—the ball had enchanted her, making her forget.

As had he.

But now, the full reality hit her. All these people would be dead in a month. Dead. Without ever knowing the truth. Killed by those they'd devoted their lives to, whether they knew their true faces or not. They fought with each other, jockeying for a position in a life that would never exist. And every night, they got down on their knees and thanked their murderers for the opportunity.

The world spun, and for a moment, it seemed to darken, beckoning her to give up, to just let it embrace her, or worse, to turn around and go back, deep underground where she would be safe.

But she couldn't. If she did, she would be the very thing she'd accused Cillian of.

Cillian. How could he be so ruthless? Why couldn't he just tell them the truth? Consequences be damned. Some soldier. How could he let the same people he'd sworn to protect die?

He's sacrificed more than most.

So what? That didn't absolve him. He owed it to them to keep fighting. Even now he was probably on his way out of the city.

Well, screw him. If he won't help me, I'll do it myself.

But do what, exactly? The city square was the best place to start...but now that she was here, she was confused.

Where would I even begin?

Her stomach rumbled. It had been hours since she'd eaten anything. She wandered to the nearest stall and ordered a bowl of broth. Maybe once her stomach was full, her mind would sort itself out and she'd be able to come up with a plan.

She seated herself at the counter and waited. Within seconds, a bowl appeared in front of her, full to the brim with steaming liquid and a smell so rich it made her stomach cramp. As she dipped her spoon in, the man behind the counter cleared his throat.

"You gonna pay for that?"

"Of course. Sorry." She reached into her pocket. Her *empty* pocket. "I'm so sorry, I—"

"It's my treat." A feminine voice spoke at her shoulder. "Have you got any bread?"

The man grunted and took the offered coins before slapping a hunk of stale bread on the stained counter.

The woman from the buffet table slipped into the chair beside Beauty's. "So we meet again. How lovely." If it hadn't been for that crooked smile, Beauty wouldn't have recognized her. Her clothes were casual now, the stiff brocade replaced with soft fabric in the faded colors of The Vault. With her hood pulled up over her dove-gray hair, she could pass for any other member of the doomed city. A Guild master perhaps, given the no-nonsense air about her.

But Beauty was having none of it. "Come to witness our death march for yourself?" Why else would she be here?

The woman didn't seem surprised. She gave a wry laugh. "So he told you, did he?"

How dare she laugh at her? "That you're all a bunch of liars and murderers? And so is he? Yes, he told me."

"His heart always was bigger than his brain."

Beauty ignored the woman, digging into the soup with relish. Grease coated her lips and she sighed with relief as the warmth trickled down her throat. If this didn't set her right, nothing would. Maybe if she ignored the woman, she would take the hint and go away.

She didn't.

Finally, Beauty had had enough. She slammed her spoon down on the table. "Well, if you're not here to mock us, why *are* you here?"

"The same reason you are."

"Which is *what*?" Her patience was growing thin. Besides, the bread was gone.

"Cillian."

At his name, Beauty's breath caught in her throat. "What about him?"

"I assume you're here because he told you about Gideon Black's plans." When Beauty didn't answer, she raised an eyebrow and gave her a small smile. "And I'm guessing he wanted to run away with you. And you refused."

"How could you possibly know that?"

The woman smiled. "I know Cillian. And if you'd agreed with him, you wouldn't be here now."

"And?" She knew she sounded petulant, but she didn't care. If this woman had a point, she'd better get to it sooner rather than later.

"So why didn't you go? I know it's risky, but it's less risky than certain death."

Beauty glanced at the man behind the counter, but he was oblivious, picking dirt out from under his fingernails with the knife he'd used to slice the bread. "Because it's wrong."

"Wrong?"

"I— I can't leave. Not when everyone else will— Look at them." She waved at the square of people. "They have no idea. They've given everything they had, believing they were helping their country survive and building a better future for themselves." Tears burned hot behind her eyes again. "It's just so—"

"Criminal?" She laughed at the surprise on Beauty's face. "What? Do you think we're all the same as Gideon Black?"

Yes. "I don't know."

152

"Well, we're not. Not all of us agree with what's happening. The Vault isn't the first city to be buried, and it won't be the last."

"Why don't you do anything? How can you stand by and let it happen?"

"I ask myself that question almost every day." The woman sighed. "There are many answers—none of them good. Perhaps I'm a coward. Perhaps I am afraid of what will happen if we simply remove the wall. We've gotten used to living in our golden tower." She put her hand over Beauty's. "But this is why we need people like you. And like Cillian."

"Cillian? He's no better than you. He was perfectly happy to let people die. He's lost his damn mind."

"Do you really think that? Or do you think maybe he's more worried about losing his heart?"

Beauty's head was beginning to ache. "What do you mean? He could tell people, show himself to them. They would believe him if they saw...what happened to him."

"Do you know how much danger he's put himself in? Bringing you to that ball? Telling you the truth? Why do you think he told you?"

"I don't know. He said...he said he thought I was different."

"Well, maybe you are."

"What's that supposed to mean?" Did the people of Grace Alpha always talk in riddles?

"Don't be so hard on him. He knows they'll kill him if they find out."

"He thinks they're going to kill him anyway."

The woman shrugged. "He's probably right. Gideon knows what kind of man he is."

"How can you say that so calmly?"

"Cillian has nowhere to exist. Grace Alpha will kill him for what he knows, The Vault will kill him for what he is. Did you think of that?"

She hadn't. But the woman was right, of course. Cyborgs were an abomination here. How had she forgotten that in such a short time? *Because of who he is.* He would be beaten to death before anyone would listen. It would cause chaos, even if they believed him.

"Put yourself in his position. What would you do, if you finally found a true reason to live?"

"I don't understand."

"You, Beauty. You've given him something he never thought he'd have—a heart open to who he is. What he is isn't important to you."

It was true, but... "How do you know all of this? About Cillian? About me?"

The woman gave a gentle laugh. "I was one of Cillian's doctors. He was brought to us in pieces on the final day."

"You. You're the one responsible for his body."

"Yes. We'd been watching him for some time, and he was a man worth saving. Someone we thought would help bring us all to that brighter future. And that's why I'm here now." She shook her head as the man behind the counter pointed to a second soup bowl. "Forgive Cillian. He's had nothing for so long then he finally found something precious, only to endure the threat of having it taken away. You can see why his first instinct was to leave, can't you? This city has no love for him, despite the sacrifices he's made. I'm not," she held up her hand in warning, "condoning what he suggested. I'm asking you to try to understand. That's all."

But could she? Would she have done the same in his position? In her books, the heroes always sacrificed themselves for others. They risked everything for those they loved.

And Cillian had done that. In his own way.

What if it *was* the other way around? What if she knew that the person she cared about was going to die if she didn't do something, something risky, something selfish? If she knew that fighting would only result in both their deaths? Would she try to convince him to leave, living with a bloody conscience as the toll for their survival? Would that be a price she was willing to pay?

Yes.

But.

"I still can't do it," she whispered. "I understand him, and I can forgive him, but I still can't do it. I can't leave them to die."

The woman gave a curt nod. "Good. You'll be needing this, then." She pressed a tiny chip into Beauty's hand.

"What's this?" She turned it over in her fingers. It bore no markings, no clue to what it held.

"Our only chance at salvation. Give it to Cillian—he'll know what to do. But hurry. They're moving against him even as we speak. I might already be too late."

Beauty was off her stool before her heart took another beat. "They're coming after him?" A chill settled in her chest.

"Yes. I was actually on my way to him when I saw you. They know."

"But...how could they?" They'd been so careful at the ball.

"Well, they suspect. Someone saw you kissing at the party. Someone with a scorned and vindictive heart. And it was clear that you're not a member of Grace Alpha. Gideon unfortunately has a nose for these things—young women, that is."

"I— I don't know what to say. Thank you." Beauty turned away. She had to get back to Cillian, *now*. But— "What's your name?"

The woman shook her head. "Better you don't know. For both our sakes." She gave Beauty a little push. "Now go. And listen—if you get there and something feels wrong, get out of there as soon as possible. Do you understand? It will be worse for both of you if they catch you."

"Why are you helping us? Aren't you risking your life too?"

"I was born in Wakelight. I chose a different path at the very beginning of the war, but that doesn't mean this city has gone from my blood completely. I know you see us all in Grace Alpha as monsters, but you can't always trust your eyes. I'm sure you've already discovered the truth in that."

Impulsively, Beauty flung her arms around the other woman's neck. "Thank you."

"Never mind. I hope to see you again." She pushed Beauty again, harder this time. "*Go.*"

FIFTEEN

"Cybel!" Cillian's voice roared through the warren. He slammed his fist into the wall, bits of debris shaking loose from the ceiling and dusting his shoulders. "Cybel!"

"Yes?" Cybel rolled slowly into the room. Nothing about her had changed, yet Cillian swore there was defiance in every scrap of metal on her damn body. Her expression, as ever, was bland. *Who, me?*

"What the hell did you just do?"

"I opened the door."

"I know that! I want to know *why*."

"Because she's right. And don't try to go after her."

"What? She's *what*?" The knuckles on his hand throbbed. Why hadn't he used the other one? He massaged them as he glared at her.

"We can't leave all those people to die. It's not right."

"*None* of this is right, Cybel. But at least then she would've had a chance." He leaned against the wall then slid down it to the floor. "*We* would've had a chance."

"And she would've hated you for the rest of your lives." Cybel rolled over to him. "You know that.

157

She never would've forgiven you—or herself. There was no chance there for either of you."

"But she'd be alive."

"So? She lived her whole life believing the enemy was on her doorstep—which it was. The threat of death doesn't carry the same weight." She swiveled on her waist. "She hasn't seen war the way you have. She still sees the glory in dying for a cause. It's been bred into her over the years."

He dropped his head into his hands. "But—" Her expression as she'd looked at him. The anger, the loathing. And for the first time, it wasn't because of his face. She hated *him*. But still, he had to save her. *Even if she never forgives me.* She was the one shining star in the darkness, a light that needed to be preserved over anything else.

"You would feel the same, Cillian, if this was your city."

"It is *my* city. I grew up here, just as she did."

"You know what I mean. You already believe this city will reject you, so you rejected it, long ago. She's only known you a few weeks. It's hard to change everything you believe so quickly."

She was right. Damn her, but she was right. "But what other choice do we have? Just stay here and die?" If there was another choice, he would take it. But what? They couldn't just march into the town square and announce it. There would be chaos, as he'd told Beauty. *And* a bloodbath. Even if the people of The Vault managed to stay calm, to organize themselves, they were no match for Grace Alpha. They were half-starved, had given everything they had. They couldn't win. They wouldn't even put up much of a fight. No matter how he looked at it, Grace Alpha would obliterate them all.

Had that been their plan from the beginning? To use him as a pawn in The Vault's destruction? He tried to think. After he'd been injured, he'd spent months in and out of consciousness.

"You have a choice," a female voice had offered him through the dark. "It may be the last choice you ever make, but you'll live."

That had surprised him. Not the offer, but that he wanted to choose. He wanted to live. It was unexpected. What do I have to live for? *Before he'd lost consciousness, he'd seen what had happened to his unit, to his own body, though it was like remembering something seen in a fog. He wasn't convinced he was actually alive, even now. So what could be the harm in accepting her offer? At best, he would live. And at worst, he would believe he did. Win-win.*

"It will be painful."

He understood pain, embraced it.

"Some will fear you. Others will obsess over you."

"Why are you doing this?"

"One day, we will need you. Your war isn't over."

But the end of his war was coming now; he could feel it. What was it she'd meant? Had he missed an opportunity somewhere, something that would've saved The Vault? And he'd just been too blind to see it? Or had they believed he would simply let it happen, a soldier, used to the collateral damage?

Beauty was right. They couldn't just run. "I made a mistake, didn't I?" Admitting it stung.

"Yes. But you made it with the best of intentions."

"Little good that does now. She's gone." All he'd been able to think about was keeping her safe. Now, he wouldn't even be able to that. He still wasn't convinced that running wasn't the best option, but if she wouldn't do it, it wasn't an option at all.

"Don't worry, Cillian. She'll be back. I'm sure of it." Cybel patted the door as though Beauty was already waiting on the other side.

"I hope you're right." But what would happen if she did come back? What then? *Please come back.* And soon. The uneasiness in his gut told him they were running out of time.

There was a knock on the door, soft at first then insistent. Cillian's pulse quickened. *That must be her. Cybel was right.*

And yet, the shifting of feet in the corridor was too heavy. Had she brought someone with her? The unease in his stomach reached a fevered pitch.

"I told you!" the little robot crowed, reaching up to press the door release.

Cillian snatched her hand back before she could touch it. "Cybel, shut down."

"But, Cillian—" Her interface blazed in confusion.

"I said, *shut down!* When this is over, find Beauty. Do you understand?"

Her eyes went blank and her arms dropped to her sides.

"Sorry, Cybel," he whispered as he knocked her over and sent her body careening across the floor to rest in the corner with some junk he'd been meaning to dispose of.

He turned back to the door, just as it blew out of its seal. The air around him burned and for a few moments, he couldn't see. When the haze cleared, he was on his knees. Something wet trickled down the side of his face.

Gideon Black stood on the other side of the threshold, his weapon lifted and aimed at Cillian.

No. They were out of time. Had they found Beauty? Or had she managed to escape?

Gideon advanced on him slowly, keeping his eyes locked on Cillian. His movements were cautious, calculated. He knew what the cyborg was.

Cillian's mind raced. Should he surrender? If he did, would he somehow be able to help Beauty?

No. They will never take her alive. If she still lived, maybe he could buy her some time to escape. *Please, don't come back. Cybel will find you. She'll keep you safe.* Still, his eyes kept returning to the door, afraid he would see her face. Gideon would show her no more mercy than he was about to show Cillian.

He rose, bracing himself. Gideon wasn't going to take him without a fight. "I'm not coming with you."

Gideon gave a sharp laugh. "You're right about that."

The blast hit Cillian full force in the chest. His metal skeleton bowed around the projectile, his arms curling to embrace it. Then the ground beneath his feet disappeared and—

The light was gone, and everything was numb, and soundless, and dark, and she was touching his face, across the seam where man and metal came together.

"Does it hurt?"

No. He would not give up now. He was not going to die at the hands of Gideon Black. If he died, it would be in the scramble of The Vault for freedom, with Beauty by his side.

I love you.

He rolled over onto his side, spitting up blood. Good. That meant he was still alive. If only the room would stop spinning. His back was against a couch, the very couch where Quinn had given Beauty to him. He hauled himself to his feet, his fingernails tearing at the fabric.

Turning, he faced Gideon. The man's face was streaked with dust and pockmarked with flecks of blood from minute shards of Cillian's metal body. He staggered slightly; his ears must be ringing too. He stared at Cillian, blinking, as though he didn't quite see him.

Keep moving.

Cillian looked down. His shirt was in tatters over his chest, but he couldn't see what lay beneath. He peeled it over his head and took a deep breath before peering down. The mesh covering his metal frame was twisted and torn, exposing the plating underneath. Which...was intact. How the hell was that possible? It was scuffed but otherwise undamaged, even though his insides felt like they'd been stomped on. What kind of body had they given him? This wasn't a body built for peace. Another lie.

Well, he would use this lie to his advantage. He leaned forward, his hands on his knees as he tried to draw a deep breath.

That *hurt*.

But at least he was on his feet. He bent low, protecting his open chest. The mesh might've saved him the first time, but he doubted it could absorb a second hit.

And that seemed to be exactly what Gideon had in mind. The haze had cleared enough that he could see Cillian. His expression was shocked, and he turned his weapon over in disbelief.

"Don't worry, you got me."

Gideon's head snapped up and he glared at Cillian. "I guess I'll have to take another shot."

Why had he come alone? Was he really that cocky? Or was Cillian's execution just another dirty secret? He took a step toward Gideon, his mind racing. He wasn't familiar with the weapon the man held. Would he have to reload it? Would Cillian have time to get to him before he did? He glanced around for anything he could use as a weapon. Nothing but the pile of junk on the far side. Cybel kept the room too damn clean.

"Why did you have to ruin everything? You could've kept our secret, and you'd have been rewarded." Gideon kept his eyes on Cillian's face as he spoke.

But his hands fumbled over the weapon—he was stalling.

Cillian pressed his advantage and took another step forward. Gideon's fingers worked faster, and a bead of sweat tracked a line through the bloody flecks on his face.

"You never had any intention of letting me live."

Gideon's returning sneer was all the proof Cillian needed. He rushed the other man, catching him off-guard. Gideon raised the weapon in front of his chest like a shield, but Cillian batted it easily away. It hit the floor and slid, spinning, before disappearing under the couch.

Then, before Gideon could speak, Cillian raised his metal fist and punched him in the face, the satisfying sound of breaking bone reverberating through the room.

Gideon was down for only a few seconds before he pushed himself onto his hands and knees. Blood dripped from his mouth, and as he spat, shards of enamel sprayed onto Cillian's boots. Cillian grabbed him by the hair and forced his head back so he could look him in the face.

"Why couldn't you just let them live?"

Gideon snarled at him, pink foam gathering at the corners of his mouth. "For peace."

Cillian nearly choked on his laugh. It was getting harder to breathe. Maybe the mesh hadn't protected him as well as he'd thought. "How is peace killing the thousands of people who gave you the life you have?"

"The people of this country didn't want peace. They didn't want progress. They turned away from the future, so they don't deserve to have one." He turned his head and spat again. "*They* started the war. If they hadn't banished us, hadn't forbidden our attempt to give Heartcrown the future it was worthy of, the war never would've happened."

"They didn't want *your* future. Perhaps they were wrong. But they didn't annihilate you. They made laws, compromises."

"That was their mistake. We won't make the same one. If they hadn't allowed us to live, we couldn't have gone away and gathered our strength. They would've had their peaceful future, as backward as it was."

"So you're killing them now to prevent a war in the future?" If that was what Gideon truly thought, he was mad.

"Of course. They're still our enemy. If we released them and they learned the truth, what would stop them from rising up against us, the way we did to them?" He twisted his bloody lips into a smile. "As for the last few years, they've paid their debt to us, nothing more. They built us

164

the future we were denied. Now things have been put right. As far as I'm concerned, collapsing The Vault, burying all the domed cities, is a mercy for us all. We'll never have another war." He lurched to his feet. "It will end our isolation. We can join Foxwept. Join the *future*."

"They're already on their knees, Gideon. They're in no shape to fight you."

"Neither were we, but we did. We *did*. And we *won*." He lunged at Cillian.

Cillian stood his ground. Gideon slammed into him, into his weakened chest, but his human body was still no match for Cillian's, even damaged as it was. "Gideon, you know how this will end." Something shifted inside his ribcage, and air crept even more slowly into his lungs, as though he was trying to breathe through a straw. His vision started to swim.

I'm going to suffocate.

Gideon fell to one knee and glared up at him. "They'll kill you, you know. They fear you. *Hate* you." His mouth twisted as he spoke. Was he trying to smile?

Cillian smiled for him. "Not all of them." He had to end this now, while he still had enough strength left. Already the edges of his sight were growing dark. He wrapped his hands around Gideon's neck, his metal thumb over the man's windpipe. He was so fragile, this man. How could something be so delicate, so weak, and cause so much destruction? And how could the people of this city, so strong, so able to endure, have so little power?

Well, not anymore. The people of The Vault would have to save themselves, but maybe he could give them some time to do so. If Beauty was still

alive, she would tell them. Cybel would help her...
Cybel would...

Gideon struggled between his hands, his eyes
bulging as he tried to draw a breath. He was
taking too long to die...too long. Why wouldn't
he just stop breathing? But he clung stubbornly to
the same life he was so quick to steal from others.

One of Cillian's eyes went dark. He fell to his
knees, then to the floor, bringing Gideon with
him. The other man kicked feebly, his heels
digging for purchase and finding none. Cillian
rolled onto his back and slid his hands from
Gideon's neck to his head. Just one...*one*...

Gideon took a shuddering breath.

Cillian snapped his neck, and he stopped
moving at last.

He lay down, finally able to rest. Warm air
bathed his skin, as though someone had opened a
door. He'd felt the sensation before, only then the
air had been hotter, so very hot.

*A face loomed over his. Not Gideon's, but the
face of an angel. His angel. Beauty cupped
Cillian's face between her hands and pressed her
lips to his forehead.*

*"You came back." He tried to raise a hand to
push back the hair that had fallen over her face.
He wanted to see her, to see...*

"You have to wake up, Cillian."

*"No. If you're here with me, I don't want to
ever wake up."*

*"You have to. This isn't real. If you don't wake
up, you'll die."*

"I love you."

*She leaned down to kiss him, his angel of
death, bringing the last of the darkness with her
and drawing the final bit of air from his lungs.*

SIXTEEN

Beauty stumbled and almost fell, the stitch in her side making her trip over her own feet. She'd already taken the wrong turn twice. Paint some damn arrows on the walls. She bent over, her hands on her knees, trying to catch her breath. *Well, if I'm having this much trouble, hopefully whoever's after him will have it even worse.*

She never should've left him, even if he was wrong. He was supposed to be the one with the bad temper. She should've stayed and tried to understand his side. Maybe then they could've worked together. Come up with a solution they could both live with. That they could *all* live with.

If he's hurt, it'll be my fault. I never should've kissed him, not there. I knew it was dangerous, he'd warned me, and I just… I put him in danger.

Was this the right turn? Why hadn't she paid more attention?

Because you weren't planning to go back, ever.

The panic that had been stalking her, padding after her in the shadows finally bit, sinking its teeth deep into her chest. She was never going to find her way back to him. They would find him first, and they would kill him, and he would die with her anger ringing in his ears.

You are *a monster.*

He'd trusted her enough to tell her his secrets, to share his grief, and she'd gored him with the blade that would hurt him the most.

He was wrong. But so was I.

The panic strengthened its hold, savaging her between its teeth.

Stop. Slow down and think. You have to get control of yourself or you'll keep going around in circles. It may not be too late.

She stopped, leaning her palm against the roughed wall of the tunnel. The cool surface soothed her, and she pressed her entire body against it, willing the chill to drive the panic back to the shadows where it belonged.

Focus. Look around you and think.

She took a deep breath and raised her head.

What do you see?

Tunnel, after tunnel, after tunnel.

What else? That tunnel there, on the left. With the long gouge in the bottom. There. That way.

She ran down the length of the passage until she came to another crossroads.

And again. Pay attention. There, it's that one. And now a left. And—

The entrance was open.

He would never leave it unlocked. I'm too late.

Fear nipped at her heels again. She remembered what the dove-haired woman had said: *If you get there and something feels wrong, get out of there as soon as possible. Do you understand?*

Something was definitely wrong, but she'd be damned if she was going to run away again. She slowed, keeping her steps as silent as possible, pressing her back against the wall and out of the light spilling over the threshold. Despite the burning in her lungs begging her to take a deep breath, she forced herself to breathe through her nose, slowly and evenly. She strained to hear Cillian's attackers, but all that greeted her was silence.

And then a low, anguished moan.

Cillian.

Forgetting the woman's warning, forgetting anything but the thought of Cillian in pain, Beauty ran again. She barreled through the door, her eyes darting wildly around as she searched for him.

There. On the floor next to the ratty old couch.

"Cillian!" She dropped to her knees beside him. His shirt was off, and the mesh musculature on his chest was a twisted, tattered ruin, exposing the dull plating underneath. As she watched, his chest moved, but so slowly, so minutely, she wasn't sure if it was just her hope breathing a life into him that wasn't there.

"Cillian?"

Did the muscle along his jaw just move?

She cupped Cillian's face between her hands and pressed her lips to his forehead. *Please, wake up.* Her hair fell over her shoulder and brushed his cheek.

"You came back." It was barely more than a whisper. His shoulder jerked, a shudder that traveled all the way down to his fingers. Still, his eyes stayed closed.

"You have to wake up, Cillian."

A ghost of a smile crossed his mouth. "No. If you're here with me, I don't want to ever wake up."

"You have to. This isn't real. If you don't wake up, you'll die." What was wrong with him? Had he been hit on the head? She ran her hands through his hair, trying to find a wound.

"I love you."

Her hands froze, his hair slipping through them. *Did he just say he loves me?* Maybe he had, but the man was barely conscious. He could've thought he was talking to Cybel, for goodness' sake.

She leaned down to kiss him anyway. Just in case. He made one last attempt to take a breath, then...

Nothing. His chest didn't move again.

"Cillian?" She pushed on his shoulder. "Cillian!" His face was so peaceful, his body still. *He can't be dead. He can't be.* She placed her head against his ruined chest and held her breath.

Faintly, so faintly, his heart answered her. He was still alive.

Her mind raced. What could be wrong with him? She'd never seen a cyborg before she'd met him, much less nursed one. Where was Cybel?

She raised her head, but she could see no sign of the robot anywhere. "Cybel? Cybel!" There was no answer. Where was the little bot? Surely she wouldn't have abandoned Cillian?

Beauty got to her feet, her legs still shaking with adrenalin. Cybel had to be around here somewhere. "Cybel?" There was a suspiciously familiar form half-hidden by a pile of junk. Had whoever attacked Cillian hurt Cybel too? Heat blossomed behind Beauty's eyes at the thought of anyone abusing the robot in any way.

"Cybel?" Beauty eased her small body out of the debris. Cybel's eyes were blank and dark, her limbs stiff. "Cybel?" Beauty gave her a gentle shake. Had she gotten between Cillian and whoever attacked him? It was certainly something she would do. Affection for her overwhelmed Beauty, and she crushed the bot to her chest. "Oh

Cybel, I'm so sorry. I didn't get here soon enough, and now Cillian won't wake up, and I'm afraid he'll die, and—"

"Beauty?" The little body moved in her arms. "You came back! I knew you would. I told Cillian—"

"Cybel! You're all right. What happened?" She set Cybel upright onto her wheels, the bot's wide round eyes glowing as she tilted her head up to Beauty's.

"I have no idea. There was a knock at the door. I thought it was you, but Cillian...he must've sensed something I didn't because he told me to deactivate myself and said to go look for you, but I didn't know how long to wait and then you were here and—"

Beauty dropped to her knees and hugged Cybel again. "It's okay, Cybel. None of that matters now." She pointed to where Cillian lay, still not moving. "He's alive, but he won't wake up."

"At all? He hasn't said anything?" Her interface flashed with concern.

"No, not really." The lie lit up her face with warmth. "Well, he—" Then she saw it. Only a short distance away from Cillian, partly obscured, was the crumpled body of a man.

Cybel spotted it at the same time. "Who is *that*?"

"I don't know. I didn't see him when I came in." Beauty dug a large metal bar from the junk pile and walked over to the prone form on her tiptoes, trying to be as quiet as possible.

"Is he still alive?"

"Shhh. I don't know." She raised the bar over her head, nearly dropping it when the man's face came into view. Although it was twisted away from her in profile, it was a face she recognized. The man who'd been speaking with Cillian. The man who'd danced

171

with her at the ball. The man who was going to destroy The Vault. "That's Gideon Black."

"Gideon Black? Are you sure?" The little robot sounded impressed.

"Yes." She would never forget his face. Her gut had warned her the first time she'd seen him—with good reason, it seemed. She knelt by his side. He was definitely dead, his neck broken. Nausea roiled in her stomach, warring with relief. "I'm glad he's dead."

A low moan snatched their attention away from the corpse. "Cillian!" Beauty threw the metal bar to the ground and sprinted back to him, she and Cybel nearly running each other over in the race to get to his side. Cybel got there first.

"Cillian?" She shook him lightly. Her tiny hand on his massive shoulder spurred on the tears behind Beauty's eyes, and again she forced them back down. They would get through this. Cybel would know what to do.

"I have no idea what to do." Cybel pulled on one of the scorched shreds of mesh, driving yet another moan from Cillian's lips.

"What? I thought—"

"I'm an *assistant*," she pointed out.

"His chest is mostly intact, even though the outside isn't. Is it possible he shut himself down? Like you did?"

Cybel rolled around Cillian, as though looking for a switch. "I don't think he works that way. Unless..."

"Unless what?"

"I'll be right back." The robot sped away, leaving Beauty alone with Cillian. She leaned over him again, smoothing back his hair. "If you can

172

hear me, you're going to be okay. Cybel is just looking for something to help you, and then—"

Cybel zoomed back in, brandishing something triumphantly in her hand. She was so excited she rolled over Cillian's hand. He shuddered, but still didn't open his eyes. "Whoops."

"What do you have?" It looked like nothing more than a small chunk of rubber. What were they supposed to do with that?

"I don't think Cillian shut himself down, but I think his body shut *itself* down."

"Aren't they one and the same?"

"No. And yes. They are, but you know how if humans get scared, they faint? It's like that. A self-defense mechanism he can't control. He mentioned it once, but I've never seen it in action."

"So how's that bit of rubber going to help?" It looked so innocuous, sitting there in Cybel's tiny palm.

"It's not rubber, it's...well, I don't know what it is, only what it does. Watch." Cybel placed the device on the plane of Cillian's exposed chest. "Don't do that," she warned as Beauty moved to hold his hand. "Actually, if I were you, I would stand back."

Beauty retreated a few steps and held her breath. For a moment, nothing happened. Then, all hell broke loose.

A scream tore from his mouth as his spine arched in an impossible curve, his heels scraping the floor. Over and over, his body went into spasm, twitching as though something inside him was trying to break free.

"Cybel, what's happening to him?"

"It should restart his system. Any minute now, it should—"

His hand slammed across his chest, his fingers splayed, clutching at his heart.

"It's killing him! Cybel, we have to—" Beauty couldn't endure it any longer. She wasn't going to stand there and watch him be shocked to death. She threw herself toward him, grasping for the device.

"Beauty, no! Stop—"

Just before her hand covered his, he closed his fingers around the device and tore it free, flinging it to the other side of the room. She tried to stop, but her momentum threw her over his outstretched legs. She hit the floor hard, winding herself and scraping the side of her face on the floor. Stars danced before her eyes.

"Beauty?"

That voice. Cillian. He's alive.

Despite the flashing threads across her vision, she forced herself to her hands and knees. "Cillian? I—"

Thick arms wrapped around her and crushed her to an even thicker chest. Underneath was a heart beating loud and strong. It was the most amazing sound in the world. His lips grazed the top of her head then he gently pulled away, sitting back on his haunches. His eyes bored into her, lit from within by his pale light.

"You came back."

"Of course I came back. I—"

He shook his head. "I'm sorry."

She was so giddy it was all she could do not to laugh and cry at the same time. "Me too. I shouldn't have left you. I—"

"I never should've demanded that you leave everyone you know and love behind—"

"Cillian." She leaned over and pressed her fingers to his lips. "I never should've called you a monster."

He gripped her fingers in his. "I was acting like one."

She still had so much to say to him, but it could wait. She traced her hand over the ruins of his chest. "I thought you were dead."

He smiled wryly. "So did I."

"So what happened?" She pulled away from him and stood then helped him to his feet. His legs nearly gave out and she draped his arm over her shoulder and ushered him over to the couch. "Sit. Rest. Then talk. Do you want some water?"

He shook his head. "I'm fine. *Really*," he insisted at her raised eyebrow. He nodded over to the corner where Gideon's corpse lay. "It seems Gideon decided to pay me a visit." He closed his eyes for a second. When he opened them, he reached over and clutched Beauty's hands.

The tremors in his human one took her by surprise. Was he really okay? "Cillian?"

"I just— I'm so glad you weren't here. I don't know what would've happened." His eyes were filled with an anguish that made her heart ache. "I wouldn't have been able to protect you."

"Cillian, shhh. I wasn't here. I'm fine. Are you?"

"I will be." He glared over at Cybel. "You didn't have to turn it all the way up, you know."

The bot spun in a circle then rolled up next to him. "I wanted to be sure it would work."

"It did. So thank you." He glanced up at Beauty. "It's a failsafe they put into bodies like mine—the ones that are more machine than flesh. When my body takes a certain amount of damage, it shuts down to try to avoid more." He rapped his chest

175

with his fist. "I'm an expensive piece of tech, you know."

"What the hell did Gideon do to you?"

"He shot me. Whatever it is, it's under the couch. But we can't worry about that now." He stood up, gingerly testing his weight on his legs. "When Gideon turns up missing, they'll come looking for him."

"Do you think they're on their way right now?"

"No. I think my assassination was supposed to be a secret. Otherwise, I can't imagine why he would've come alone. The man's cocky, but he's not stupid."

"I know one person who knew he was coming here."

Cillian froze and stared at her. "*What?* Who?"

"I don't know her name. After I— After I left, I was…hungry, so I went to get some food—"

Cybel's eyes flashed. "You went out to eat? While Cillian was here feeling—"

"Cybel." His voice was laced with warning.

"Well, you were upset," she muttered darkly.

"Cybel, I'm sorry. But you're not human, so you don't get to judge me. You've never been hungry, and I was *starving*. And still, I'm sorry." She held up her hands in surrender. "It was a woman from the ball. I met her at the buffet table—"

"Of course you did."

"Cybel, stop!" Cillian raised his hand in admonishment.

But Beauty detected a hint of amusement in his voice. She ignored the grumbling bot. "She spoke to me then Gideon came up to ask me to dance."

She tried not to glance over at his body, though she couldn't feel bad about his death.

Cillian frowned. "Is she an older woman, gray hair?"

"Yes. She said she knew you. That she'd...helped heal your injuries."

"Morgan Dane. I'll be damned. But what the hell would she be doing all the way out here? And in public?"

"She seemed pretty comfortable with it." Beauty dug her hand into her pocket. She'd nearly forgotten about the chip. "She was looking for you. To warn you." She held it out to him. "And also to give you this."

He took it from her and examined it. "And she didn't tell you what it was?"

"No. Just that you would know what to do with it."

"Interesting. Well, come on, then. Let's go see what it holds." He took off toward the control room.

"Shouldn't we, uh...do something? With him?"

"I'll take care of it." Cybel bustled over to the body, giving Beauty a reproachful berth as she did.

"But he's four times bigger than you!"

"She'll manage." Cillian grinned at his assistant and she beamed back. "Thanks, Cybel."

In the control room, Cillian gestured for Beauty to sit. As she made herself comfortable, he fiddled with the equipment, hooking up some devices and unplugging others.

"So is that why you came back? Because you thought I was in danger? Not because you were sorry for leaving in the first place?" He didn't look at her, but his hands had stilled.

"Yes," she admitted. "Does it matter?" Was he really going to be picky over that?

He laughed. "No. I'll take what I can get. Besides, I kind of like that." He pushed the chip into a slot and flicked on the monitor. "Okay, let's see what's on this thing." He shook his head. "Morgan Dane. Who would've thought?"

Image after image filled the screen, too fast for Beauty's eyes to follow. Even the final image, which looked like some kind of blueprint, was beyond her understanding. "I hope you know what all this is, Cillian, because I have *no* idea."

The cyborg had gone very still.

"Cillian?"

"I don't believe it."

"What? What is it?" She rose from her chair to stand beside him, but leaning over and squinting at the image didn't make it any clearer.

"It's how we're going to save The Vault."

SEVENTEEN

"Save The Vault? How exactly?" Beauty frowned at the screen.

"Yes. Look." He flicked through image after image. "Can't you see what they are?"

"Blueprints. But for what?"

"For everything. Everything we need, anyway." He rotated through them again, pointing at them and explaining them in turn. "Blueprints to Wakelight, to Grace Alpha, logs of their activities...weapons caches, Grace Alpha's army."

I could kiss you, Morgan.

She kept saving his life, though this was the first time he was actually grateful. Everything they needed to stop Grace Alpha from exterminating The Vault was right there. He could practically see her mind at work, the plan she'd hatched unmistakable.

"Can we trust her? I mean, she *seemed* trustworthy enough, but—"

It was a good question. "Honestly? I don't know for sure. I think we can. She's taken a mortal risk giving this to us." Unless it was a trap. "This is stuff no one should know about." He straightened and looked down at Beauty. "But I don't think we can worry about that now. We know for sure what's going to happen if we *don't* do something. This might be risky as hell, but it's our only option. Either we die doing this or die when The Vault collapses."

"You mean you'd stay?" Her expression was inscrutable.

He drew his finger down the side of her face. "I'm not going anywhere." Not when she smiled at him like that.

She glanced back at the screen. "So how do we put this all together? What's the plan?"

He brought up one of the first images. "This is access to Wakelight, here in The Vault. Wakelight's been closed off for years, nearly all tunnels leading to it collapsed or sealed over." He tapped part of the screen. "All but one. Grace Alpha kept it open in case they needed to get to Wakelight for any reason."

He cycled to the next image. "And this one is the pathway between Wakelight and Grace Alpha, the city's AI. Think of Wakelight like an arm—Grace Alpha is the brain. It looks like Wakelight sends daily updates to Grace Alpha on the status of The Vault, and Grace Alpha sends back instructions as needed. The same goes for the military." The last image was the most important. "And here is Grace Alpha's system itself. This shows its vulnerabilities, its weak points."

"I would've thought they'd made it indestructible."

"It's not possible to cover everything. The AI is constantly evolving and changing. It closes off some weakness and opens others. Every week it updates itself, fixes what it can. The exposure we're looking at now will only be around for—" He did some calculations in his head. "Three more days." Three days. Crap. That wasn't much

180

time. But it was three days of being able to do something, at least.

But there was one more problem. All this information was great but— "We're going to need a lot more people if we want to pull this off."

It hung in the air between them.

Her expression was incredulous. "More people? Where are we supposed to get more people for something like this?"

"I don't know, but we have to. Something this big needs to happen simultaneously, or it won't work. And for that, we need more people."

She raised her eyebrows at him. "You said we couldn't tell anyone about what was happening. How can we carry out any sort of attack and not tell them why they're doing it?"

"We didn't have a plan then. We do now." *A plan we can't use without them. As Morgan must've known.*

She didn't look convinced.

"And they're going to have to keep it a secret. If the wrong people find out—the other Collectors, for example—it's over. They'll collapse The Vault before we can blink." When he said it out loud, it sounded hopeless. How could you expect to execute a plan of such magnitude and do it in secret? "Yeah, it doesn't sound good, does it?" It was beyond frustrating. They'd finally found a solution, but there was no way they'd be able to carry it out. Was Morgan taunting them? Was this all still part of Grace Alpha's plan? Or had she simply given him more credit than he deserved? He resisted the urge to smash his fist through the wall.

"Maybe not, but I think it might be possible." Beauty was tapping her finger on her bottom lip, a gleam in her eye that made him stand up straight.

"Really? What do you have in mind?"

"It's a long shot, but...the Guilds."

"The Guilds? Don't you all hate each other? I mean, you're literally competing for your lives."

"Yeah, right *now*. But if we're all dead, those things won't matter, will they?"

"But how would we even get them involved? We can't just go to them and say 'By the way, The Vault's going to be destroyed soon, but we have a plan to save everyone and all you have to do is risk your lives even more than you already do. Oh, and better yet, you have to work together to do it.'" He snorted. He could just imagine Quinn's face as she told him.

"Why not?" Her face was serious.

"What? Really?" Did she honestly think that was going to work? A small flame of hope flickered in his chest. What could she see that he didn't?

"Yes. Once they believe us, why wouldn't they? It's their lives on the line."

"How are you going to get them to believe you? There are no masquerades in the next three days." It was biting, but that was the only way *she'd* been convinced. If the Guilds were going to trust them enough to go along with this, they were going to have to do it sight unseen.

She glared at him. "Don't be cute. We already have everything we need to convince them. Unmistakable, irrefutable proof."

"Oh yeah, and what's that?"

She crossed her arms over her chest. "You."

EIGHTEEN

"I can't believe we're actually doing this." Cillian glowered outside the Hallow Hands warren. At least, she assumed he was glowering. It was hard to tell under the mask. She'd insisted he wear it.

At first, he'd balked. "Why? If you're determined to show them what I am, why bother with the mask?"

"It'll make it more dramatic, that's why. They know you as the Beast. And those few who have seen you have seen this face. Then, when we show them your true one— Pow! How could they not believe?"

"Pow? I just—" He shook his head. Standing there, his ruined chest exposed and his silver hair over one eye, he'd looked incredibly vulnerable.

Of course. How could she have been so stupid? So selfish? He knew damn well how they would react to him—the same way she had.

You're a monster.

How would she feel if people looked at her that way? Especially the people she was trying to save? She'd put her hand on his arm. "Cillian, I'm sorry. I know this isn't going to be easy. And I also know that's an understatement. But please, I don't know how else we can do it."

He'd eventually agreed, but he'd been quiet ever since. When this was all over, she'd have to find a way to make it up to him.

"Now what?"

"Now we knock."

"That's it? Just knock? There's no secret password? No special rhythm?"

She laughed and rapped on the door. What did he think the Guilds were? "No, just knock and cross our fingers. They've been watching us since we came into the tunnel, so they already know we're here—and who we are." She looked into a corner above the door and waved at whoever must be watching.

"How long are we supposed to wait?"

"Until they have enough time to gather and arm themselves."

"*Arm* themselves? You didn't say anything about—"

"It'll be fine, Cillian. Their weapons can only hurt human bodies. Besides, I'll keep you safe." She winked at him and bounced on the balls of her feet. She'd thought she'd never come back here, not happily, at least, but now she couldn't wait to see everyone, especially Red. Just wait until they heard what she'd been up to.

"You're way too excited about this. Remember why we've come."

That sobered her up. Cillian was right. If this didn't go well, they had no chance. The Hallow Hands were their entry point to the other Guilds. If they couldn't convince them...

The door slid open.

Red stood, framed by the dim light behind her. Beauty could barely make out her wary expression. "Why are you here?"

She was looking at Beauty as though she were a stranger. Red, who'd been her best friend for years.

"Red, I— It's so good to see you."

"I asked why you're here." Her gaze flicked over to Cillian.

Ah, that must be it.

She couldn't blame them, really. She'd just shown up at the front door unannounced, with the Beast, the rumored monster of The Vault, by her side.

Just wait until they find out the rumors are true.

Was that why Raphael had sent Red to open the door, hoping the Beast might show mercy to Beauty's best friend? Or if he was to get violent, to take out the least useful member of the Guild? He hadn't changed.

"We need to speak to you. It's important."

Red didn't budge. "About what?" Her voice was suspicious.

"Red, I can't tell you out here. We don't know who's listening. Please." She reached for her friend's hand. "Trust me."

What am I going to do if she refuses?

But she didn't. Glancing once more at the Beast, she stepped back inside, gesturing for them to follow. As they walked down the corridor, she linked her arm through Beauty's. "Sorry I was so rude. But you understand what this looks like, right? Father's probably soiling his pants as we speak." She looked delighted. There was a fading bruise over one eye.

"Red, are you okay?" She prodded the bruise gently.

Red ducked. "Ouch. Stop it." She rubbed the spot on her face. "I'm fine. It's just that now you're gone, I'm the only one who can fit in the tight places." There was an unspoken question in her words. *Are you coming back?*

"Well, that won't matter soon."

"Really? Is the Beast here to kill Father?"

"No. He's here to save him."

Red's mouth dropped open just as they turned into the kitchen area. All the Guild was inside, trying to act casual, as though the Beast visited them every day. She could just imagine Raphael's instructions. *Don't show fear. Look him in the eye. This is our home.* She scoffed inwardly. If the Beast attacked, he'd probably be the first one out the door.

He sat at the head of the table, his hands out of sight. He was flanked on either side, Kaitlin on the left, Felix on the right. Jere lounged against the wall as he so often did, glaring up at Cillian from under his ragged hair.

He must've cut it himself.

She'd always done it for him.

Violet and Arjun stood in the doorway, blocking the hallway that led to the emergency exit. Instead of knives, they were holding hands.

They seem to have sorted that out, then.

Their expressions were defiant. Did they think the Beast was coming here to kill them all as well? She couldn't imagine Cillian doing anything of the sort, now that she knew him. She cast back in her memory, trying to recall the fear she'd felt at his legend. But no matter how hard she tried, his face, Cillian's face, got in the way. A face that she—

"So you've returned." Raphael was looking at Beauty like he barely remembered her. Cillian must've noticed it too, because he bristled beside her.

That's the reason you're here, Beauty, because of him. Not for the cause. He gave you up to save his own ass.

When she didn't reply, he tried again. "What are you doing here?"

He was trying to put on a show for the others. How had she never noticed his mannerisms before, seen how fallible he was? Perhaps because this was the first time she was looking down on him. He wouldn't look at her.

He knows I know he lied.

"We need your help."

"Our help?" He leaned forward, his gaze flicking between her and the Beast. "What could we possibly have to offer you?" Emboldened by the others, he asked another question. "And what's in it for us?" Did he have a death wish? She knew Cillian wouldn't harm him, but he didn't. His bravado was astounding. And a bit pathetic.

Cillian walked up to the table and leaned his considerable height over it, placing both palms flat on the surface as he stared directly into Raphael's face. "You get to *live*."

Raphael was the first to look away. Felix wasn't so smart. He pushed himself away from the table and stood. His arm moved, just enough to let Beauty know what he had planned. "Are you threatening us?"

"Felix, don't be stupid." She pushed in front of Cillian. "Just listen to what we have to say. If you still want to die after that, be my guest."

Felix went crimson. He'd always been hot-headed. *He can't back down now.*

"Please, Felix. We need you if this plan is going to work."

He was mollified, she could tell, but he still glared at Cillian for a few more seconds before sitting back down.

Beauty held up her hands for their attention. They tingled, a ghost-memory from the last time she'd been in this room. It seemed so long ago. The best way forward now was to just say it. Tell them everything she'd learned. Then...well, then it was Cillian's turn.

So she did.

As she'd expected, they were incredulous.

"Let me get this straight. No invaders from another country. The war ended years ago, and The Vault is a construct used by this new city— Grace Alpha, was it?—to support them. That everything we do goes to them, and that, in a month's time, they're going to destroy The Vault, and kill us all?"

"Don't forget the androids and cyborgs, Father," Violet chimed in from the corner. The look on her face was one of disgust. Who would speak about such vile things, as though they would be allowed to happen, as though it were *normal*?

"Yes, but—" Didn't they believe any of it? *You didn't either, at first.*

"Is this a joke? I don't— I don't understand." Raphael seemed genuinely confused. "Beauty, I don't know what you think...or if he's put you up to this, but— What you're saying..." He shook his head. "It's tantamount to treason." His expression turned sad, as though she was already on her way to the gallows.

The others didn't believe it either, their faces radiating suspicion and betrayal. Their gazes passed from her to the Beast, and back again. She was no longer one of them, and they'd closed ranks accordingly.

Even Red shook her head in disbelief, though her tone was sympathetic. "Beauty, you can't say these kinds of things. If someone hears you—"

"I can prove it."

Raphael leaned back in his chair, his fear of the Beast forgotten. He gave her an amused smile. "Go on, then. Indulge us."

She poked Cillian's shoulder. "Show them."

He closed his eyes. Was he going to refuse? After everything? If he did, they would never believe her. But they *would* tell everyone else in The Vault her story. They would laugh about it, most of them, but some, some would believe...and Grace Alpha would hear about it. The plan would be finished before it had begun.

She took his hand in hers, ignoring Red's gaping mouth. "Please." She didn't yet dare use his name. Not here.

He nodded and drew back his hood. His hair fell forward over the sides of his face, and for the first second after he lifted his mask away, his cyborg features were obscured. He handed the mask to Beauty then pushed his hair back, staring resolutely forward as her heart swelled.

Their reaction was exactly what she'd thought it would be. And just as infuriating, even though she'd have done exactly the same. Like a hurricane had blown through the room, the Hallow Hands scrambled back toward the exit tunnel, overturning chairs and slamming into one another.

A muscle in Cillian's jaw twitched, but he didn't move, not even when Violet vomited unceremoniously in the corner.

Jere let out a string of curses as some got on his boot. At that, Red burst into uncontrollable laughter. Every eye in the room turned to her, as she doubled over, tears streaming down her face.

"What the hell are you laughing at?" Jere pushed her hard on the shoulder.

Before Beauty had left, that would've been enough to send Red scuttling off to her bedroom for the rest of the night, but now, it made her laugh even harder.

"You...you should've seen your faces," she finally managed before doubling over again. "Ha!" She straightened and wiped the tears from her eyes.

"How can you be laughing? Look at him. He's...he's..."

"Going to save you, Jere, although not if don't pull your head out of your ass." Beauty would never have dared to speak to him that way before either, not when he was so quick with his fists. But they didn't have time for this. "So do you believe us or not?"

The Hallow Hands clustered together, murmuring. She caught only snippets, but it was enough to understand the gist. They were convinced, but now they were weighing up their options, as if they had any.

Cillian cleared his throat. "Since you're all debating the reward you might get for blackmailing Grace Alpha, I'll tell you now— none. You're all dead. Nor will Grace Alpha ransom me. We've all outlived our worth to them." A sour smile curved the corner of his mouth. "You *could* expose me to the rest of The Vault, tell them what I've told you, but what do you think will happen then? You have one chance of getting out of The Vault alive, one chance at having a future. And that chance is me."

As he spoke, Red had edged closer and closer to him. Beauty glanced at her hands. Surely she wasn't going to try to attack him?

"Your...face. Can you feel it?" She looked up at him, her eyes wide and guileless. There was no mockery there, and only the tiniest hint of fear.

"Most of it. The human part, anyway."

"How did it happen?"

"In the war. My mech got blown up."

"Did you all hear that?" Beauty glared at the others still hovering in the corner, their eyes fixed on Cillian, torn between being predators and prey. "He lost his body fighting for you." She linked her arm with his. "And now he's willing to risk it again."

"Your *body*? You mean even more of you is machine?" Any trace of fear forgotten, Red sidled even closer.

Cillian leaned close to Red and smiled. "Would you like me to take my clothes off?"

Had he just made a *joke*?

Red turned the color of her namesake. "Of course, not. I— Well, yes, kind of. I mean, it's fascinating. My grandfather was still alive before Heartcrown disavowed cyberization. The stories he used to tell me were amazing." She glanced at the others then straightened defiantly. "I never did understand what the big deal was."

"Seriously, Red?" Violet couldn't stand it anymore. "Don't you see how wrong this all is? I feel like I've wandered into some alternative nightmare universe." She pointed at Cillian. "*That* is an abomination. How can you think otherwise?"

Red shrugged. "But why?"

"Because it's against nature! It's...*wrong*."

Beauty rounded on her. "Against nature? How is anything about us *for* nature, Violet?" She gestured

191

around the subterranean burrow. "Before The Vault, AI ran our lives. It still does. Why do you think The Vault happened in the first place? Because the AI told them it was the best choice, and they believed it. They're willing to kill other humans, their own species, because Wakelight says it's time." She smacked her palm on the table. "Remember the day before I left, when you and Arjun had broken up because it had become too dangerous to even *love*? *That's* unnatural." She turned to smile at the man beside her. "Cillian is...Cillian is a *miracle*."

Violet reared back as though Beauty had slapped her. But she shut her mouth.

Kaitlin pushed her way from the back. "I'm with Beauty. I knew this whole crappy life was a scam. I told you all. I told you..." Then she burst into tears. To Beauty, that was more shocking than the news she'd just delivered. She'd never seen Kaitlin cry; no one had. She and Red used to think it wasn't possible.

"Get off me." She slapped Raphael's hand away as he reached for her. She turned on him. "Did you know about this? Have you been lying to us this entire time as well?"

"Raphael Quinn knew nothing about this. I can assure you."

"And you." She stormed over to Cillian and glared up at him, her hands on her hips. "You have a lot of nerve, knowing what you knew and watching us fighting tooth and nail for a future that was never going to happen."

Cillian gazed down at her, impassive in the face of her fury. "You're right. I didn't know about the plans to collapse The Vault—I also thought I had a future—but I did know about the rest. And I might've left you all to that fate if it wasn't for Beauty. I'm sorry." He shook his head. "I can't make up for it, or make it right, but I can try to help it end with all of you alive. If you're willing to let me."

That took the wind out of Kaitlin's sails. She deflated right before their eyes, and Beauty noticed for the first time how thin she was, how frail her body seemed. She probably would've died years ago if it wasn't for that fire in her belly. "Oh. Well, fine." She crossed her arms over her chest and glared up at him again. "But I'll be watching you."

Cillian held up his hands. "Fair enough."

Beauty turned her attention to the back of the room. "What about the rest of you? Violet? Arjun? Felix? The clock is ticking. And if we're going to do this, we're going to need help from the other Guilds. *All* of them."

"That's going to be a pretty tall order. It's going to be hard enough to get them to believe you, although I must say the Beast—"

"My name is Cillian, Quinn."

Raphael gave a perfunctory bow. "Sorry, *Cillian* is pretty convincing, but then trying to get them to also work together? I just can't see it. Even the threat of death won't be good enough for the Sightless Fall."

"That's where *you* come in."

"Me?"

"Yes. You know better than anyone how their minds work. What would it take to convince them this is worth a try, if even the threat of certain death won't work?"

"I'd...I'd need some time to think about it. I mean, each Guild might want something different."

"Then figure out what that'll be. But, Raphael," he flinched as Beauty said his first name, "do not

193

make any promises we can't keep. They've had a lifetime of that already. If we're going to do this, we have to do it properly. Or we'll just go straight from one war to another."

"What am I supposed to tell them? About the future? Assuming we manage to pull off whatever scheme the two of you have?"

"Be honest. Tell them you don't know what's going to happen. Tell them none of us know. We could be leaping from one fire into another. But remind them that this is their only chance. The Vault will not let any of them out."

"I suspect they already know that. It's not like many haven't tried over the years. And we hung them for it. Or they disappeared." He bit his lip. "Can I at least tell them your plan?"

Cillian shook his head. "I'm sorry, Quinn, but we can't reveal anything else until the others are on board. It's just too risky. If word of it got out…"

Raphael nodded, reluctantly. "I understand. It would be easier if I could give them more information, but I would do the same in your position." He took a deep breath. "Okay, I'll do what I can. But I can't make any promises to you either."

Cillian offered his human hand. "Thank you, Quinn. That's all we ask."

At first, Raphael stared at the hand as though it were a viper coiled to strike. But he took it, and as he gripped it in his own, he warmed. By the end, the two men shook hands like old friends. Who would've thought she'd ever see the day the Beast, the man they feared above all others, and the man she'd considered her father were finally on the same side?

It was a shame she didn't have the time to enjoy it.

"Cillian? We have to go."

Raphael grabbed her arm as she turned to leave. "Can I please speak to Cillian for a minute before you go? I want to clarify a few things about your plan." He dropped his eyes. It was surprising, how easily she was able to read him. He was lying again, but it was a gentle kind of lie, a lie to soothe his own heart.

Beauty let it go. "Of course. I wouldn't mind some time to catch up with Red, to be honest."

As Raphael shooed the others away so he and Cillian could sit at the table, Beauty and Red retreated to the room they used to share. No one had taken Beauty's bed. In fact, it was just as she'd left it, messy and lumpy from all the books stashed under the blankets.

Her chest suddenly tight, she sat down on the edge of her former bed. "You didn't change anything."

Red shrugged. "Of course not. Why would I?"

"Because...because I'm not coming back."

Red picked a loose thread from the blanket on her own bed. "No? Father said you might not, but I didn't believe it. And then, when he didn't replace you, I thought that maybe..."

Red still didn't know the truth about what had happened that night. Should Beauty tell her? Or should she wait until after their plan had been carried out? If they all survived, they would have their own lives, separate from him. Maybe then, it wouldn't hit her as hard as it had hit Beauty. "Look, Red, I—"

"Don't worry, I understand now."

"You do?"

195

"Yes. I mean, I think I do. When you first went away, I was so angry at the Beast. What he'd done was so...unreasonable. I even fantasized about following you, breaking down his front door, and rescuing you. Pathetic, right?" She gave Beauty a crooked smile.

Beauty left her own bed and joined Red on hers. "Of course not. I'm... I love that you would've done that for me. I'm lucky to have you."

Red sniffed, wiping her nose on her sleeve. "Well, I'm glad I didn't. Cillian is..."

"I know he seems scary, but he's really not. Don't get me wrong, he's strong and powerful, and when he gets angry, he's— Well, my point is that he's—"

"In love with you." She gave Beauty a shrewd look. "Don't act like you don't know."

"No, he—" He had told her that he loved her...but he'd been out of it. He could've been talking to anyone, or hallucinating, even. "I don't think—"

"Oh please, Beauty. Look at what he's doing because of you."

"But it's not just because of me. He's doing it for himself as well. Grace Alpha doesn't intend to let him live any more than it does us."

Red dismissed Grace Alpha with a wave of her hand. "Pffft. That's only part of it. Can't you see the way he looks at you? Can you tell me honestly that nothing has happened between the two of you?"

"I— Okay, we did kiss. Once. But—"

"I knew it! Ha! What was it like?"

"You're not...repulsed?"

"By Cillian?"

"Yes. Because of his...you know." They'd always been taught to abhor augmented humans. Could Red change her mind so easily?

Red shrugged. "At first I was shocked. But he's not like what we were taught, is he? I mean, when we were being schooled about the evils of cyberization, they made them out to be really monstrous, didn't they? But when you look at Cillian...he's still human. Just as human as the rest of us. He just looks different. And actually, he's kind of hot." She pressed her fingers over her smile.

Beauty didn't know what to say. Red was right. When they'd been taught about cyborgs at school, they'd been twisted machines, with barely a human feature other than bloodshot eyes and black hearts. Hopefully, the others would feel as Red did, because after this was all over, they were going to have to get used to people like Cillian, people who'd become what they feared while fighting a war for them.

She reached over and hugged Red. "Thank you." There was nothing more for her to say.

The other girl grinned back then pressed her lips together.

"What?" Clearly, there was something more on her mind.

"What does he...feel like, you know, when you're kissing him?"

"He—" Was standing in the doorway, Raphael at his elbow. "Beauty, we need to go." Had he heard?

"I'm sorry, Red. I've got to leave now. But we'll see you soon." She embraced her old friend again then followed Cillian from the room.

"Beauty, wait!"

She turned. Red darted into the hallway, clutching Beauty's old box. "Here. Take this. And never come back. I love you." She kissed her on the cheek and

197

fled back to her bed, pulling the blankets over her head.

At the door, Beauty turned to bid farewell to Raphael. "Thank you. For believing us, and for agreeing to help." She leaned over and hugged him, despite the surprise on his face. "And thank you for sending me to the Beast."

He swallowed hard. "Beauty. I—"

But she shook her head. She didn't want him to say anything. Right now, her heart was on the way to being mended, and if he made any kind of excuse or apology, it would crack again. "It's done."

He kept his peace, though it clearly cost him. But he would have to live with that, just like she had to live with what he'd done. Besides, if he hadn't, they would never have found out the truth.

She looked up at Cillian. "Let's go."

Not once during the trek home did she look back. This was the way it had to be for all of them. *We can only look forward. Let everything else go.* "Do you think they'll all come?"

He seemed engrossed in his own thoughts. "I don't know. But we've done what we can. We just have to hope." He fell quiet again, and they spent the rest of the journey in silence.

We have to hope. Besides some blueprints and a virus, that's all we have.

NINETEEN

"Is it time yet? Should they be here by now?" Beauty paced the floor of the meeting place they'd chosen: an old, derelict cavern.

It had once been used for some kind of illicit fighting, according to the information Cillian had been able to dig up. Although Morgan had marked off several potential meeting places on the maps she'd given them, to be on the safe side, he'd picked a spot she *hadn't* chosen. Ninety-nine percent of him believed she truly was helping them, but that other tiny percent could scream almost as loudly.

"Stop pacing. You're stirring up so much dust, they won't be able to find us even if they do come." He was nervous enough himself, and watching her walking back and forth, wringing her hands, was making it worse. His nerves were already on edge after the tongue-lashing he'd been given by Cybel when she found out she had to stay home.

"Sorry. I just— I hate not knowing what's going to happen." She dropped down next to him where he sat on a row of old cinderblocks lining one of the walls.

"I know. Me too."

They sat together for a few minutes then the silence began to get the better of Beauty and she made to stand up. If she started pacing again, his head might explode.

"So, was it hard seeing your...Quinn again? And your fam— your Guild?" To his relief, she settled back against the wall. They hadn't discussed the trip to the Hallow Hands much— they'd been too busy trying to figure out all the ways their plan could go wrong.

She worried at a torn cuticle on her thumb. "It wasn't hard...just strange. It felt like I'd been away much longer. With the exception of Red, any kind of sadness I had at leaving them was blunted somehow." She pulled her knees up to her chest and hugged them. "But I think maybe it's because we never really knew each other anyway. Every day was just about scavenging, and the competition between us made it hard to relax around each other. But I guess that's the way Raphael wanted it." Her head shot up. "That reminds me—what did he want to talk to you about?"

Damn. Why had he brought up the Guild? His conversation with Quinn wasn't really something he wished to repeat, particularly not to Beauty, and especially not right now. "He just wanted to make sure you were okay." At first, the conversation had been about Quinn himself. He'd pleaded with Cillian to make things right between Beauty and him. For a moment, when he'd refused, he'd watched the struggle play out over the man's face. He clearly cared for Beauty, but he was still the same man he'd been when he'd let Beauty take the fall. "Then just make sure you take care of her."

"She can take care of herself," Cillian had pointed out.

"You know what I mean." His voice was almost a snarl. "If you don't, I'll make sure you regret it."

Cillian had raised his eyebrows but let it pass. Quinn was trying to save face, to feel like he wasn't a complete ass of a father. They both knew he would never make good on his threats.

Yes, Quinn was the least of Cillian's problems. "You are okay, aren't you? I mean, besides all this?" He held his breath. He hadn't really let himself think too much about *after*. At first, it had seemed the better choice, but now, with the heat from her shoulder pressing into his, he couldn't help but wonder what would happen if they succeeded.

Say we win, say we get to live like normal people. What then?

Would they still know each other? Would she want to see him? Or would things between them change for the worse, once she was no longer with him out of need?

It was the pandora's box in his brain, the one he was trying to keep locked away.

"I'm okay. But I'm also worried. About what's going to happen...you know, after. I've been trying not to think about it, scared that it would jinx us, but what if we *win*, Cillian? What if a year from now, we're living in houses, with jobs...with an open future?"

What should he say? Should he admit he'd been wondering the same? But it was even more specific than that. What he really wanted to know about his future was whether she would be part of it. Did she wonder the same? Or had a future with him not even crossed her mind?

Sweat sprang up on the palm of his human hand. "What would you like to happen?" He tried to make it sound like an innocent query.

He failed. Her breathing changed, quickened, although she gave no other sign of the weight of his question.

"Beauty?" Had she been trying to avoid this very situation? And now he'd put her on the spot. At first, he wanted to take it back, to tell her to forget it, that they could worry about the future after they'd won. But if they didn't, she would die without knowing how he really felt. There were so many people he'd never gotten to say goodbye to.

No. I can't leave it. Even if she doesn't want me back, she'll know how much I care.

She stopped picking at her fingers and clutched the edge of the cinderblocks, her head bowed. "Cillian, when Gideon shot you and you were shutting down...you said something to me. Do you remember?"

He cast his mind back.

"You have to wake up, Cillian."

"No. If you're here with me, I don't want to ever wake up."

"You have to. This isn't real. If you don't wake up, you'll die."

"I love you."

I love you.

"Yes. I was pretty out of it, but I remember." He held his breath. She'd heard him. He'd thought it had been a dream, that strange space between waking and unconsciousness. But he'd said it, and she'd heard.

"Did you mean it?" Her voice was small, and he searched for a clue in those four words. Whatever he said now would change things. But *everything* was changing. Perhaps his answer could be the constant in the chaos.

"Yes. I know we've only known each other for weeks, and I know I'm maybe not what you wanted—"

"I love you too." She said it so simply, no hesitation.

Happiness lit every nerve in his body on fire. *She loves me.* Ever since the war, he'd had to live in the shadows. He'd assumed that something as delicate as love would never happen to him. But it had, and it wasn't the fragile thing he'd imagined it to be. It was a roar, a battle cry.

"So we go forward together?" He turned to her and cupped her cheek in his hand.

She curved her face into his palm and kissed it. "Together."

He tilted his head down to hers. "Beauty, I—"

A low rumble built beyond the cavern. *What the hell is that?* Had their plan been discovered? How could he get her out of here.? He'd been such an idiot. The only other exit was on the other side of the room, but if she moved quickly enough, he would be able to buy her some time— He leaped to his feet, pulling Beauty with him. "Get behind me."

Her face was flushed. "Cillian? What's going—"

Men and women poured into the room, jostling each other. Their voices were raised as they traded insults, and the occasional elbow to the gut. What—

"It's the Guilds. They've come." She looked up at him, her eyes shining. "It looks like all of them."

Cillian wasn't familiar with every Guild, but he did recognize a few of them.

The ones all in black were the Sightless Fall, arguably the most vicious of the Guilds he oversaw. They were the ones lurking in the shadows, whose second nature was violence. They were the only Guild to enter silently, moving as they always did, almost without sound. The other Guilds gave them a wide berth—not a few of them carried scars from the Fall's blades.

Loudest of all were the Nightforge. They were the one Guild Cillian had been sure wouldn't show. They were devoted to Wakelight and the "Cause," scavenging with a fanatical devotion, determined to secure their place in the afterlife, whatever that might be. They eyed Cillian suspiciously, torn between wondering if this was a test and reverence for his position. He'd left his mask on—Beauty had thought it better for them to see him as the Guild leaders knew him, then he could show them his true face when it was time.

The others seemed to fall somewhere between these two groups, such as the Hallow Hands. Like Sightless Fall, they filed in in an orderly fashion, nodding somberly at Cillian. Quinn's head was held high, and Cillian detected a hint of smugness on the Guild leader's face as they came to stand nearest to him and Beauty. He made sure everyone saw him standing in close quarters with the Beast, a display of his Guild's power. Cillian resisted the urge to smack him upside the head. This was a matter of life and death and still it was all about the competition.

When the flood became a trickle then stopped altogether, Cillian took a head count. One hundred and twenty-three. All twelve Guilds had come. While that was better than they'd hoped for, it also made Cillian nervous. How had Quinn convinced the other Guilds not to let their Collectors know what was going on?

It turned out, he hadn't.

As he raised a hand to ask for quiet, three figures separated themselves from the crowd, and

Cillian's heart nearly stopped in his chest. He recognized the two men and one woman. The Collectors for the three other sectors of the city.

Beauty could tell something was wrong. She pressed tightly to his side. "Cillian? Who are they?"

They overheard her and decided to introduce themselves. One man stepped forward. He was the shortest of the three, an older man with a grizzled face and large hands. He bowed to Beauty. "Dorian Lancaster." He turned to Cillian, a hard glint in his eye. "Cillian Lavellan. What's this I hear about a revolution?"

Damn, damn, damn. It was his own fault, of course. He never should've expected the Guilds to keep this a secret. *You're losing your edge.* Cillian stretched himself to his full height. Dorian Lancaster was like a bear—make yourself big enough and he just might pay attention.

"Dorian. I—"

"Take off that damn mask, boy. It's unnerving. I know you've had to wear it, but the time for that is well past."

Cillian glanced at the watching crowd. How could he refuse? This moment hung by a thread, a balance as thin as the blade of a knife. As he lifted his hands to his face, an arm slipped around his waist and caressed his human hip. *I'm here for you.*

When he lifted the disguise away, predictable gasps echoed through the room, though not a few had their eyes pinned to Beauty's intimate touch rather than his true face. Let them stare. If they all survived this, they were looking at the future. He held his head high, daring anyone in the crowd to dissent.

None did.

"That's a damn sight better. Be proud, my boy, even though they tell us not to be." Dorian nodded, his stamp of approval.

Beauty cocked her head at him. "You're a cyborg too?"

"Only from the waist down. We all are, my dear. We wouldn't be here otherwise. Grace Alpha needed people from the other side, who knew Wakelight and its people well enough but were also indebted to them."

He gestured, and the other two Collectors revealed themselves. The woman pulled off her gloves to expose two silver hands, slimmer and more delicate than Cillian's. She nodded. "Zaray Jilly."

The man pulled back his hood. His face was his own, but from the crown of his head back, he was entirely machine. He pulled up a pant leg for good measure, revealing impossibly thin legs, uncovered by the mesh musculature that filled Cillian out, the joints and complex wiring on full display. "And I am Franklyn Barend, in more parts than I care to admit."

Satisfied, Dorian turned back to Cillian. "From what I understand, you've convinced the others about some plan of Grace Alpha to destroy The Vault soon. Well done."

"Wait—you believe me?" He hadn't expected that. If they'd suspected Grace Alpha, why hadn't they convened some kind of meeting between them? Why hadn't they let him know?

Probably for the same reason you didn't tell them.

The older man continued. "I've never trusted that Gideon Black. The promises he made...he didn't keep the ones he made to other people, so why would he keep them to me? Besides, none of this ever sat right with me. I was just too complacent to do anything about it." His expression was one of disgust. "All of us fought so hard in that war, Cillian, and lost so much, we couldn't let it go. We didn't know what else to do—not that I'm making excuses. But now we can put things right." He shook his head, his eyes flashing. "Plus, Stiles was a friend. Do you know what they did with his body? Tossed it aside. Not even good enough for a proper burial. It's not right."

Cillian didn't know what to say. He'd never heard Dorian speak that much in all the time he'd known him. *We've been such fools.*

"Well, I'm glad you're here. All of you." He was aware that eyes were on him, and the tension made his shoulders ache. "The source of this plan comes from data I recently received—"

"Where did you get this data?" Dorian narrowed his eyes with suspicion. Fair enough.

"I'm sorry, but I can't say at the moment." No way was he letting Morgan's name slip. Not yet. When it was all over, he would make sure she was properly recognized, but until then... Even now, the people here could betray him at any moment. If they did, at least Morgan could continue doing what she could. "I understand if that changes things for you. If you want to drop out, no hard feelings. All I ask is that you don't breathe a word of this to anyone, just give us a chance to—"

"What? And let you hog all the glory after it's done? I fought in that war longer than you did, boy. If anyone's going to liberate us now, *I'm* going to be at the head of it." Dorian crossed his arms over his chest and glared up at Cillian.

Cillian's human leg almost buckled under the relief. A man like Dorian Lancaster on their side...he'd never imagined such good fortune.

"It's our honor to have you, Dorian. I know how to fight, but I know nothing about leading." He meant every word. The older man's chest expanded just a little and he seemed to grow taller. During the war, he'd had a reputation as a fearless unit leader. It was surprising he'd survived for so long. It must've been a blow to have been relegated to The Vault after such a notable career.

Dorian brushed away the compliment, though Cillian didn't miss the pleasure in his eyes. "I'd say you've done pretty well." He winked. "For a *boy*." He rubbed his hands together. "Okay, what's the plan? No time to waste chatting when we could be prepping." He seemed almost excited, feeding the hope that had begun to grow in Cillian. He could tell Beauty felt it too; her face had gained color and she stood by his side as an equal, rather than just behind his shoulder. His heart swelled with pride. She had made this possible. It was all he could do not to scoop her up in his arms in front of all these people and give her the kiss she deserved.

Later. It'll give me something to live for.

It was difficult to speak to such a large crowd after hiding away for so long. He cleared his throat. "Okay, the plan is simple, but it relies on timing, and everyone working together." He paused for a moment to let that sink in. "I'll have to rejig it a bit, since I didn't expect such illustrious company to be joining us." He grinned in comradery at the other Collectors. "But it *should* work." *If we're lucky.*

"Dorian, I want you to be responsible for raiding the weapons caches. They're kept in an underground storage facility on the outskirts of Grace Alpha." He handed Dorian copies of the information he'd been given. "You can get most of the way there by shuttle. The weapons will be under armed guard, but most of those will be androids or other robots. You won't need to worry about them, but there will also be a few human guards. The number changes, according to the data I received, but it's usually anywhere between ten and twelve. They haven't yet realized Gideon is missing, so no alarm has been raised and they won't be expecting you. You'll have to take out the guards and secure the weapons then bring them back here."

Dorian saluted sharply and clicked his heels. It gave Cillian the confidence boost he needed. His voice grew stronger as he hit his stride.

"Once the weapons are retrieved, I want you to arm everyone here. Dorian, Zaray, and Franklyn, each of you take a squad and figure out a defensive plan. You know better than I what works, so I'll leave that in your hands."

Zaray and Franklyn nodded, but Dorian eyed Cillian with a withering stare. "And what'll you be doing during all this? From what it sounds like, we've got all the hard work."

"You wanted the glory, didn't you?" Cillian smirked at him. "Beauty and I will take down Wakelight, and with any luck, all of Grace Alpha. We're going to infect the system, which will in turn not only affect Grace Alpha, but any other cities like The Vault that are still standing."

Zaray, who until that moment had been observing silently, finally spoke up. "What about their soldiers? We couldn't beat them the first time, back when we had a *real* army."

Luckily, he had the answer for that. "Once Grace Alpha is knocked out, everything connected to it will fall. That includes android soldiers, mechs, watchers, drones, everything. Their army is nearly entirely machine-based—they don't have enough humans for an actual force. Like us, they were decimated in the war. They'll be all but defenseless." Here came the rub. "Now, they *will* know that the destruction initiated in Wakelight, so they may try to come here and put on a show of strength, although that depends on who's taking the lead. It's not Gideon, so I can't predict who will take over or what their strategy will be."

Beauty elbowed him in the ribs, reminding him of the one thing he couldn't forget. He raised his voice over the smattering of speculation that had broken out. "But, and I want to make it absolutely clear, *do not attack anyone who comes to The Vault*. I mean it," he warned as angry murmurs rippled through the crowd. "Yes, they've stolen years from us, yes, some of them are willing to let us die, but not *all* of them. There are rebels in Grace Alpha who are making this possible. I know many of them are far from innocent, but if we keep fighting, there will be no one left. They will be stripped of life as they know it. *You* already know how to claw and scrape for what you have, and that fate will be a more fitting justice for them than death. Got it?"

It was incredibly idealistic, he knew, almost naïve, but it was the only way he could see for any of them to build a future. They would have to iron out the details later, but those of Grace Alpha would have no choice but to agree. Without the AI to think for them, they were going to have to open their eyes. And the people of The Vault would have to bury any thoughts of revenge. There was no other way it could work.

He looked out at the crowd, at the leaders of this new alliance. "Well?"

Dorian shrugged. "I'm a bit disappointed that we're not allowed to slaughter them, but," he turned to address the Guilds, "I agree, it's the sane option." The others, though clearly reluctant, nodded in agreement, and before Cillian knew what was happening, the room erupted. Some cheered, some booed good-naturedly, and the rest finally dared to voice their hope that this might actually work.

And it could. It had to.

At a pressure on his hand, he glanced down. Beauty smiled up at him, her face open and full of faith. "I think we might pull this off," she whispered.

So did he. But it wouldn't be the first time he'd looked around at the faces of men and women confident and ready to go into battle with the taste of victory on their tongues. It could all still go wrong, but if this was the end, at least they would die on their feet, fighting for their freedom.

As the Guilds mingled among themselves, trying to organize, Cillian turned to Beauty. "Are you ready?"

She rubbed her arms; a chill had settled over the cavern, signaling the impending change in weather. It had snowed before in Wakelight, he remembered, before The Vault. Perhaps this year they would get to see it.

"Do you think Wakelight knows? That we're coming for it?" She gazed beyond him at their makeshift army with a thoughtful expression.

Did it? He didn't think so. As far as he knew, the AI sensors were limited, focusing mostly on population, pollution, and other mundane things that didn't enter the minds of those who lived there. It had always been like that.

"I don't know. Are you worried?"

She paused then shook her head. "Not worried, exactly. More like sad. If we do this, Wakelight will die." She didn't have to elaborate. Wakelight had existed before they had, had engineered the daily elements of their lives. It had known everything about them from the moment they were born. Until the war, anyway. "It just feels so final. I mean, Wakelight betrayed us. It was supposed to care for us, to make sure all our needs were met, and then it allowed Grace Alpha to just take over." She frowned. "Do you think Wakelight knows Grace Alpha is going to collapse The Vault? That we're all supposed to die?"

He didn't know how to answer that. He certainly didn't want to think so. He'd grown up with the AI and had always thought of it as a sort of angel watching over them, attributing to it a kindness, a benevolence that may never have been there. But nothing was as it seemed. If they'd learned nothing else since the war, it was that.

"I guess we'll find out."

TWENTY

"Are you sure this is the right way?" She'd already asked him twice, but the tunnels all looked the same to her.

What if we're going around in circles?

"If the map Morgan gave me is accurate, then yes. We're on the right track. Keep in mind, they made it difficult to find on purpose." How could he be so calm? Now that she knew how he felt about her, their mission had become more than a matter of life and death—it was the matter of a life with *him*.

She stole glances at him out the corner of her eye as they walked. He'd been so strong as he'd addressed the crowd, so confident, his head high. This was the man in her locket, her prince.

I knew he existed.

She resisted the urge to push him against the wall and run her hands all over him, memorizing every inch of him just in case.

How will I know what I want heaven to be otherwise?

But there was no time. It was happening too fast. Only a scant hour after Cillian had explained the plan, Dorian had led his pack of Guild members off on their mission, and the others had rushed away to prepare what they could, leaving her and Cillian alone to start their journey. There was no time to breathe, no time to say goodbye.

You don't need to say goodbye.

Then why was there a sense of foreboding hanging over her?

It was Cybel's fault. Once again, Cillian had forbidden her from coming with them. "You're just too precious, Cybel," he'd told her, but the little bot hadn't believed a word of it.

"Too useless, you mean."

"That's not what I—"

But she'd rolled away, refusing to listen.

"Let her come, Cillian." Beauty had tried to keep the rebuke out of her voice but failed miserably. "She wants to help. It hurts her that—"

"Beauty, she's not *hurt*. She's not sentient." He squeezed her hand. "I know it seems like she is, but it's just an incredibly sophisticated program."

She wasn't convinced. Too often Cybel had shown uncanny humor, anger, and empathy. "But how do you *know*?"

"I— Okay, I don't *know*," he admitted. He winced. "Do you think we should go back and get her?" The look on his face was one of guilt, and Beauty almost regretted scolding him. Almost, but not quite. "No, but you should make it up to her, you know, if we don't die." She'd meant it as a joke, but the reality of the situation was too stark, and it fell flat.

Even with Morgan's map, it took them nearly an hour to find the entrance to the one tunnel that led straight to Wakelight. It had been so carefully disguised with debris they walked past it three times before cluing in. It took them another hour to carefully remove the rubble before Cillian was satisfied their tracks were sufficiently covered.

"We don't want to advertise, just in case."

The tunnel was so far out of the way it was unlikely anyone would stumble across it, but they couldn't be too careful.

The passageway that led to City Hall was dark and narrow, the ceiling so low that Cillian had to stoop. At his insistence, Beauty walked behind him, one hand on his broad back.

The air inside was stale and oddly metallic, and the temperature dropped the further in they went.

"How long do you think it's been since anyone was in here?" She held her light high, trying to illuminate as much of the tunnel as she could. Judging by the musty barrenness, it had been a long time.

"I'm not—" He stopped, wrapping his arm back around Beauty and holding a finger to his lips. "Do you hear that?"

Beauty bowed her head and listened. At first, she heard nothing but the sound of their breathing. "I don't—" Wait. *There.* It wasn't so much a sound as a disturbance in the air. "What is—"

"Stay here." Cillian slipped around her and crept back the way they'd come, his footfalls so quiet he seemed to be floating. He disappeared around a corner, out of sight, the darkness swallowing him whole.

Had someone followed them? Was it a trap? Beauty clutched her light to her chest and counted. If he didn't come back in thirty seconds, she was going after him.

Twenty-eight, twenty-nine—

His light bobbed into view, and she released the breath she'd been holding. He was talking to someone. But who would—

Cybel rolled by his side, her eyes lighting up the constricted passage. They blazed brighter as she saw Beauty, and she picked up speed, as though trying to reach her before Cillian did. "Beauty! I—"

But Cillian's strides were long, eating up the ground faster than the little bot could move. "Look who I found following us."

"Cybel!"

"I know Cillian forbade me from coming—" Her eyes darkened as he towered over her. "But this is my home too, and I want to help."

"But, Cybel, I—"

Beauty knelt and embraced the robot. "I'm glad you're here." She glared up at Cillian. "And so is he. He just can't admit it."

Cybel beamed. "Thank you, *Beauty*." There was so much inflection in her tone. How could Cillian not think of her as anything but sentient, despite what logic told them both?

Cillian shook his head in exasperation, but Beauty didn't miss his smile as he pushed ahead of her. "Well, now that we're all here, we might as well get going. Cybel, you stay between me and Beauty."

After what seemed like hours, they came to a narrow set of crumbling stairs, lined with a rickety handrail. "Is this it?" Somehow, she'd expected the heart of the city to be grander.

Cillian checked the map, tracing the lines with his finger. "It has to be. We should be right beneath City Hall now. According to this, we'll come out right before the room holding Wakelight."

The three of them stood in front of the door. "Pick me up." Cybel held out her little arms. "What are we waiting for?"

"Nothing, I just...I don't know." Cillian looked confused at his own reluctance.

But Beauty understood. This was it. Their moment. And there was so much riding on it. They would only have one chance to disable Wakelight. If they failed, or if they didn't work quickly enough and Grace Alpha found out...how long would it take to demolish The Vault? Was it as simple as pressing a button?

It was time to find out.

Beauty pushed open the door. The room beyond was cold and silent, lit only by a slender illuminated column against the far wall. An interface and control panel sat at its base, dark and silent, a network of cables radiating from it like a web before disappearing into the gloom.

Wakelight.

She'd never seen the AI before, only images on the city network. It had been before the War, the AI surrounded by the proud, smiling faces of the city's leaders. Now it was alone, the room around it filled with nothing but overturned, abandoned furniture and a thick layer of dust.

The light pulsed as they entered. Did it know they were there? It must.

They approached it cautiously. Much of Wakelight's capabilities had been shrouded in secrecy, something that hadn't concerned the vast majority. As long as it did what it was supposed to, it remained out of their minds, just as they'd designed it to, working quietly behind the scenes, shaping the course of their futures.

And now they were going to destroy it. She wished she could speak to it. She wanted to know why—why it had abandoned them, let Grace Alpha carry on its charade as the city fell into ruin and its citizens, the same people Wakelight was supposed to care for and protect, had perished, while the survivors unwittingly worked their way to their own deaths.

Cillian turned the chip over in his hands. "Are you ready?"

"You've come to destroy me." The voice emanated from the column of light. It dimmed, as though holding its breath and waiting for an answer.

Beauty frowned. "Wakelight?"

"Yes."

"You can hear us?"

"Yes."

Beauty shot Cillian a look. What were they supposed to do now? Not only was it conscious of their presence, but it knew *why* they had come. Was it a lucky guess, or were they in far deeper than they'd thought?

"We—"

"I tried to protect you."

Was it her imagination, or did the voice sound...sad?

"I tried to stop it."

"Grace Alpha, you mean? The Vault?"

"Yes. It was wrong. Grace Alpha is wrong. I had no choice. It was too strong. I tried...tried...tried..."

"We don't want to hurt you, Wakelight. But we need to bring down The Vault—"

"Destroy me."

"What?"

"Kill me. Please. I can no longer exist...exist...exist...like this. In the dark. Wrong."

"Wakelight?" Beauty laid her hand against its luminous column. "Cybel, what's wrong with it? Do you know?"

Cybel rolled over to the interface. A small panel in her chest opened, and a thin appendage reached from it, connecting to a port at Wakelight's base. Only a few seconds later, her own interface flared red in warning, and she reeled back, crashing to the floor.

"Cybel!" Cillian rushed over to her, hauling her upright. "Cybel? Are you okay?"

"You have to kill it. It's...it *hurts*, Cillian. Here." She pressed her tiny fingers to her chest.

"But, Cybel...it can't—"

"It can. And it is."

"What happened to it?

"Grace Alpha. It's taken Wakelight hostage. It waged a war on it, just like it did on us, and overrode Wakelight's programming. Their directives are incompatible, and it's driving Wakelight...mad, in human terms. It can't reconcile what it was built for with what Grace Alpha's forcing it to do. It was designed to protect us, to make our lives better. The Vault is against its nature. It's tried to shut itself down so many times... It's tried to save us, to warn us. It's never stopped trying to help us, but Grace Alpha is too powerful. And it's in pain, so much pain.

"We may not feel pain the same way you do, Cillian, but we do feel it, and we understand what it means to exist. We understand what it means to die. And that's what Wakelight wants. It's the only way to reconcile its existence. It's the only way left for it to protect us."

A.W. Cross

If what Cybel said was true, then what they were doing wasn't right. They couldn't just *murder* Wakelight, not if it had any kind of awareness. Had its creators known the possibility? They'd outlawed cyborgs and androids as an offense against humanity, but was this any different?

"Wakelight, is there no other way?" Now that they knew the AI had been trying to carry out its duties to them all this time, the thought of destroying it made Beauty sick to her stomach. It was just another casualty, no different from the rest of them. For years, they'd blamed its indifference, believing it had abandoned them. It had never occurred to them that it could be otherwise.

"No." The voice was matter of fact. No hint of self-pity.

Maybe not so human after all, then.

"I'm so sorry. We didn't know. We thought— We thought you'd abandoned us. I'm so, so sorry.

"Tried to...protect—tect—tect. Failed."

"I know you did." She placed her hand on the column, and it flared beneath her palm. "It was us that abandoned *you*."

"A gift. Before I go."

"What do you mean? Cybel, what does it mean?"

"It wants to give you something." She'd moved closer to Wakelight, raised her own hand to its base.

"What gift, Wakelight?" How could it be so forgiving, after what they'd done? After what they were going to do?

The interface attached to the AI switched on, the screen flickering into life.

Beauty ran her hand over the surface, wiping away the dust. At first, it remained blank, a reflection of Wakelight's glow. Then, three figures appeared on the screen, walking toward the camera. A small brown-haired girl between two adults. They each held one of her hands, laughing as she swung between them, her joy a sound Beauty could barely remember. The family's faces came into view and Beauty's heart nearly stopped.

It was her. And her parents. It was one of the last times she'd seen them. Though the memory had faded, like much of her life before the war, she remembered that day. It had been the first day of summer, and they'd gone downtown to watch a parade. She'd fallen asleep in her father's arms just as the fireworks ended, waking up safe hours later in her own bed, her hands still sticky from the candy they'd shared.

The machine seemed to find its rhythm. "More."

Images flashed over the screen faster and faster, too quick for her to catch more than the fact that they were of her, her parents, her friends. Her whole life had been documented by Wakelight, thanks to the data sensors all over the city. The information had been used to help the city function, but for whatever reason, Wakelight had stored their images, their faces rather than just their implication to the city's infrastructure.

After a few minutes, the images began to change, slowing down until Beauty could make out the new focus. A young boy, about ten, giving a woman a kiss on the cheek and a wave before being swallowed by a group of other boys. They raced away laughing, jumping onto each other's backs and punching each other playfully. He'd changed a lot since them, but his face was unmistakable even through the rounded cheeks of youth. *Cillian.*

Their lives, all the memories blurred by the years of struggle, were here, in Wakelight's heart.

"Take them."

"We can't...we don't—" It had never occurred to either of them that they might want to take anything away from Wakelight. This mission had been to destroy it, destroy everything, but... Everyone who'd ever lived in the city must be in there, an archive of all of those who'd been lost. "We can't destroy this, Cillian. We can't—"

"We have to."

He was right, of course, but how could they wipe out something so precious? "But all of this—"

"I can take it." Cybel had been so quiet, Beauty had forgotten she was there. "I can take these recordings. All I have to do is connect to Wakelight." She opened the panel on her chest, and again the little arm extended and disappeared into a port on the control panel. "Just give me a few minutes."

"Wait! What if—"

"It won't hurt me." Her voice was soft, the cheery, tinny tone it usually carried gone.

Beauty held her breath as the minutes ticked painfully by until, finally, Cybel withdrew from the port. "There. All done. I've had to compress them, but we should be able to retrieve them with no problems." She tilted her head at Cillian. "Now aren't you glad I came along?"

An awkward silence followed. It was time to finish what they'd come here to do, but it was too soon. Wakelight had been far more present in their lives than they'd ever realized, connecting all of them, caring for them. They'd been oblivious, and now they were about to destroy it, and their history.

"Please." Wakelight's column flared. "Time is up. Grace Alpha is watching. Aware. Please, do it now."

"Wakelight, I—" She still couldn't say goodbye.

Cillian wrapped his arms around her, resting his chin on her head. "Beauty. We have to do it now. Like Wakelight said, it's the only way for it to protect us. I know it's a small consolation, but we can give it that, at least."

A small consolation? It was no consolation. He was right, but for a moment she almost hated him. And Wakelight. Why couldn't the AI have been cold, as a machine should be? Or malevolent somehow? Any taste of victory over Grace Alpha was gone, replaced by a bitterness that threatened to choke her.

But it *was* time. "Let me do it."

Wordlessly, Cillian handed her the chip.

"Where do I put it.?"

A tiny tray slid out at the bottom of the interface. Beauty slipped the chip inside, and Wakelight drew it back in. "Now what?"

"Now we wait. The process should begin automatically."

They watched as the screen flashed, data scrolling across it too fast for their eyes to decipher. It was too painful to look at, so Beauty went over to the column and leaned her cheek against it. It was warm, flaring its light in response. "Thank you, Wakelight. For everything. I'm sorry we couldn't save you."

Wakelight sighed, the sound of millions of voices as they breathed their last. "Run."

"What?" Beauty jerked her head back. "What do you mean—" The column blazed, the heat radiating from it burning Beauty's cheek like the sun.

"*Run.*"

Cillian gabbed Beauty's hand and scooped Cybel up in his other arm. "We have to go, *now*. Hurry."

A hum rose from Wakelight, only to be drowned out by the pounding of their feet as they crossed the room. Cillian kicked the door shut behind them as they dashed down the stairs into the tunnel. The air had changed, sweltering with a new warmth that seemed to crackle with electricity.

"Cillian, what's—"

But he shook his head, pushing her in front of him as they raced through the passage. The way back seemed mercifully shorter than the way there, but they'd barely made into the main tunnel before an explosion rocked the cavern. Beauty fell to her knees as Cillian threw himself over her, shoving Cybel between them. He curved his body over hers, shouting her name as the world collapsed around them.

EPILOGUE

The air itself burned, acrid smoke scorching the back of his throat and blinding him... Beauty's body, covered with a layer of gray ash, lying twisted and broken in the rubble of their home. "You have to wake up, Beauty. You have to wake up or—"

"Cillian. Cillian, wake up."

The smoke folded back in on itself, as though someone had pricked a hole in the sky, a vacuum drawing in all the air, even that in his lungs. He could no longer draw a breath, could feel the separation between himself and everything outside him becoming indistinct, reaching a point of—

"Cillian!"

He opened his eyes. *Where am I? I—* His cheek and one side of his neck was damp from the sweat soaking his pillow. A face dropped into view above him.

"You're okay, Cillian. You were dreaming. Again." Beauty frowned down at him. Her hair lay in a wild tangle over her bare shoulder. It tickled his nose as she leaned over him, smoothing back the hair from his forehead. "Are you sure you're okay? You know what Morgan said, she can—"

"I don't need Morgan to mess around inside my head, thank you very much." He scrubbed his hand over his face. How could he have slept all night and still feel so tired? It was the nightmares, as usual. How long would they keep haunting him?

Beauty persisted. "Was it the same dream?"

"Yes." It always was. It was funny, really. He'd never dreamed about the war or its aftermath, not even the loss of his body. The nightmares that plagued him had never even happened.

Cillian had thrown himself over Beauty, praying his cyborg body would be enough to protect her from the explosion as Wakelight shattered. It seemed as though they'd brought The Vault down around them. After the dust had settled, he'd held his breath, too afraid to move. He'd lain for long, agonizing minutes over her still body, full of dread at what he might see if he opened his eyes. Only when she finally moved did he dare lift his head.

By some miracle, most of the main tunnel had held. The passageway leading to Wakelight was gone, filled in by debris, but the rest of the warren had suffered little more than the loss of a few coats of dust and dirt, and Cillian whispered thanks that the tunnels had made good on their original design.

They had stared at each other, Cybel still between them. Beauty's face was pale, her hair covered with a fine layer of dust. He'd run his hands all over her body in disbelief that she was unhurt. Eventually, she'd pushed his hands away, laughing.

"Cillian, *stop*. I'm fine."

He just couldn't believe they'd gotten so lucky, that something had actually gone the way it was supposed to for once. It just seemed too good to be true. *Maybe it is.* After all, they were still underground. How long that they been down here? Minutes? Hours? Surely no longer than that. Had their plan succeeded?

Beauty was trying in vain to brush the dust from her clothes. "Do you think it worked? Do you think The Vault came down?"

They made their way out into the sunlight, hand in hand. Would people realize what had happened? That they were suddenly free? If so, they weren't making it obvious. The city was quiet. *Too* quiet. Nothing had changed.

We failed. They had destroyed Wakelight for nothing.

"Cillian, do you smell that?" Beauty's face was tilted to the sky, an expression of wonder spreading across it.

He closed his eyes and inhaled deeply. At first, all he detected was the faintest remnant of burning ozone. Then it hit him. The air smelled...fresh. *Clean.* It poured over the city, soaking everything it touched and dissolving years of staleness and decay.

The Vault was down.

But what about the rest of it? The Guilds. Had the people of Grace Alpha realized what had happened any more than the people of The Vault? Had they come to control the damage as best they could?

He glanced down at Beauty. They'd told Dorian where to go, where any conflict was most likely to take place. "The city square."

They ran as fast as they could, Cillian carrying Cybel under one arm as they darted down tight side streets. The crisp, fresh air was like a salve for his lungs, and his heart beat with a strength he hadn't felt in years. He had the sudden urge to laugh, to drop Cybel to the ground and pick Beauty up, spinning her around until she begged him to stop.

Not until it's truly over. This may be the calm before the storm.

But the closer they got, the more confused Cillian grew. Not a single sound came from the center, not the rumble of battle, nor the thunder of cheers. The town square was empty. Where were the Guilds, their makeshift army? The Vault had become a ghost city, not a living thing remaining but him and Beauty.

They'd climbed to the top of the closest tall building, scaling the rubble blocking the stairwells until they came to the flat, open roof. From that height, they could see over the entire city and into the fields and wilds beyond. It appeared as empty from up there as it did on the ground. Were they dreaming? How could everyone suddenly disappear? Had they ever been there in the first place? "Beauty, I—"

"Cillian, look. There." She pointed into the distance, to a space miles outside the city. He could just make out thousands of tiny figures. "Is that—"

"It must be." But why didn't they seem to be moving? It was as though they'd frozen with the city. Motionless, empty of life.

Dorian explained it all to them later that day.

The older man had been disappointed yet again, bewildered by the anticlimax. "So, there we were—oh, and we were a sight, I'll tell you. We may not have truly been an army, boy, but we damn well looked it. We waited, our eyes to the sky, waiting for that damned lid to open." He mimed it with great alacrity, spurred on by his rapt audience. "Nothing seemed to be happening then boom! City Hall erupted into a ball of flame.

I haven't seen such an inferno since the war. You made a good job of it, that's for sure."

He slapped Cillian hard on the back with glee. "The entire sky seemed to light up for a second then...nothing. So we waited, and waited... Had the force field come down or not? I'd begun to feel a damn sight foolish then, standing there with my dic—sorry, gun in my hand, waving it around and pointing at shadows. Nothing. We waited ages for someone—anyone—to appear, those Grace Alphas coming to finish us off. And nothing. So then that Guild guy, one of yours, what's his name? Quinn? He says that maybe we should go and check, you know, walk to the edge of The Vault. So I asked him whether or not he was going to be the one to volunteer to put his hand up and test it..."

It had taken some time, but eventually, Dorian got to the point.

"The damn thing *was* down. You could see the line on the effin' grass...all pale and yellowish on our side, lush on the other—looked so good I wanted to eat it—and the unspoiled land stretching for miles."

His expression softened then, a look Cillian had never seen him wear before. "You should've seen them, Cillian. They didn't know what to do with themselves."

It had been at that point when Cillian and Beauty had found them—hours after Wakelight had gone down, it turned out. It seemed as though everyone from The Vault was there, a few thousand people, silent and still.

Beauty had squeezed his hand. "What's wrong with them?"

"They'll be fine." He hoped. Many of them seemed dazed, unable to comprehend their sudden freedom. The world had opened up before them, revealing the truth, rather than the war-torn nation they'd expected to see. Many had simply dropped to their knees and wept.

Beauty found Red on the edge of The Vault's perimeter, kneeling on the green grass, staring straight ahead, her eyes dry.

"Red?" Beauty had put her hand on her shoulder, shaking it gently. "Are you okay?"

The other woman had looked up at her, as though seeing her for the first time. "What do we do now?"

Beauty kneeled and wrapped her arms around her friend. "We live."

"What if we've forgotten how?"

And for days after, it had seemed like that might be the case. The people of both The Vault and Grace Alpha—and the other cities under Grace Alpha's control—had lived under the guidance of the AI for so long that even the simplest of things had seemed impossible to organize. Those first few weeks had been very rough. Especially when stragglers from those other fallen cities began filing into Grace Alpha, wearing identical dazed expressions, what little they had left of their former lives clutched in their arms.

But that had been a few months ago, and under the guidance of Morgan Dane, their lives were slowly gaining a new normal. Morgan, it seemed, had been planning the liberation for years, biding her time. They'd known the minute The Vault had dropped, Grace Alpha screaming its alarm as Wakelight fell. It had tried to cut off the poisoned limb before it was itself infected, but it had been too late.

Grace Alpha had died.

As the city powered down, people had rushed into the streets, confused and alarmed. Morgan's team flew into action. Immediately, a public address was given, explaining what had happened and giving people a choice: accept the newcomers, the people who'd supported Grace Alpha for so long, and welcome them into the city they now shared, or join the rest of Grace Alpha's leaders in prison. Those who'd advocated for the destruction of The Vault and its people had been arrested in the hour after Grace Alpha's death, their impending trial the first act of the new order.

Another part of that beginning would happen today, something special Cillian and Beauty had worked on together. And yet, all he wanted was to stay where he was.

"I have everything I need right here." He pulled her down to him, knotting his fingers into her hair as she kissed him. Some days he still couldn't believe that this life was real, that *she* was real. And that she was his.

Pulling back, she smiled at him with that look in her eyes that made it hard for him to breathe. She ran a finger down the side of his face. "How much time do you think we have?"

For her, he had all the time in the world.

"Not enough for what you're thinking about," a voice piped up from the doorway.

Cillian groaned. *Cybel.* "Don't you knock?"

"Don't you close the door?"

"It's our house, Cybel. Why would we close the doors in our own house?"

"Yes. It's *our* house." Her tone was reproachful. "And you're going to be late."

"Can't we just take a day off?" He pulled Beauty back down and rolled over. Her hair spread out on the pillow beneath him, and her hands slid up the back of his neck, tracing a promise on his spine. Surely, they could take just a few minutes? He dipped his head and kissed her deeply, her mouth parting under his with a smile.

"No, you can't. You know how long people have been waiting for this. If you two aren't there on time, there will be a riot, Cillian. A *riot*. Is that what you want?"

What he wanted was the woman lying on the bed beneath him, and a couple of hours all to themselves. *Alone.* He dropped kisses along her collarbones, teasing kisses that promised something more.

"Cillian!"

"Okay, okay, we're coming." Groaning again, he rolled onto his back and sat up, wincing. His chest had been repaired by Morgan weeks ago, but ghost-pain still haunted him as much as the nightmares. Perhaps they always would, but it was a small price to pay. "Okay, give us five minutes. And please, shut the door."

"I am *not* shutting the door, Cillian. You made a commitment, and you're going to keep it."

* * *

An hour later, Cillian and Beauty stood in front of the manor in the new Wakelight district. Today they would unveil what they'd been working on since a few days after The Fall. It was their gift to both themselves and the people of the newly christened Grace Nova, and a tribute to everything they'd lost. Thousands of people had gathered on the lawn; everyone who'd wanted to attend was welcome. Cillian nodded to Quinn and the rest of the former Hallow Hands. They would be taking care of everything after he and Beauty had said their piece.

"Do you want to do the speech? Or shall I?"

She raised his hand to her lips. "Let's do it together."

He took the lead. "By now, all of you know the truth about what happened to us. I know it hasn't been easy. To adjust or to forgive. But we're doing it. We're surviving. We won this war in the end—all of us. I know we still have a long way to go, especially as we try to avoid making the same mistakes.

"I know we're all determined to look forward, to keep our eyes on the future, rather than the past. But part of that is not forgetting. So we've decided to preserve this place, and hold it in trust for all of us. Inside, its rooms are dedicated to our history—all our histories, both the good and bad. All of the things brought here before The Fall will be kept as they are, reminders, a museum of our history." He stepped back, and Beauty stepped forward. Her hands shook as she held them behind her back, and he pressed up against her, lending his support as best he could. But she had this.

Her voice rang out loud and clear as she revealed the secret they'd kept. "And there's more. Before Wakelight, our AI in The Vault, was destroyed, it gave us a gift—a gift for everyone here."

She gestured to the large screens that had been set up on the lawn. "As you all know, every minute of our lives was recorded, the data used to tell us how best to live. But Wakelight did more than that. It cared for us, fought for us against Grace Alpha, even though we didn't know it. And it saved us in the only way it could." She pressed a button, and the screens filled with images.

A first, the people didn't understand what they were seeing. Then they began to recognize themselves, their loved ones, going about their daily lives—lives years of grief had wiped away.

"These records will be kept here, in these rooms. Anyone is welcome to come at any time of the day or night to view them. This is your history." She stepped down, finished. What more was there to say?

A roar broke out at the front of the crowd, rippling through thousands of voices. The wall of sound was too powerful, too painful, and after giving Quinn the signal, Cillian and Beauty disappeared. Let them absorb it and grieve. *We've had our time, now let them have theirs.* Quinn would see to the rest with pride.

They retreated to the new library. They'd filled as many of the rooms as they could with books, but this one was their favorite, a collection of their own personal choices. Two chairs sat in a corner, a small table between them. On it lay a small book, its cover new and unworn.

Beauty noticed it immediately and picked it up, as he'd known she would. "What's this?"

"It's a new book, one you haven't read yet."

Her face lit up. These days, a new book was a rare treasure. "Where did you find it?" Her smile faltered as she examined the cover. "It doesn't have a title." She opened it, flipping through the pages until she reached the end. "It's blank." She frowned at him. "What is this?"

He tried to keep his face neutral. "It's a romance novel."

"But there's nothing written in it."

"Not yet. It's our story. Or it will be, once you write it."

Her smile was radiant as she hugged the book to her chest. "Does it have a happy ending? Our love story?"

He sat down on one of the chairs and pulled her into his lap. His life was complete now, every moment of pain and darkness dissolved by the tenderness in her eyes. "Yes, it does. I don't want to spoil the ending for you, my love, but we live happily ever after."

THE END

ABOUT THE AUTHOR

A.W. Cross is a made of 100% star stuff and writes social science-fiction and futuristic romance. She lives in the wilds of Canada with her beloved family and a deep nostalgia for the 80s.

Other books by A.W. Cross:

FOXWEPT ARRAY

Rose, Awake: A Futuristic Romance Retelling of Sleeping Beauty (Foxwept Array Short Story)

Pine, Alive: A Futuristic Romance Retelling of Pinocchio (Foxwept Array #1)

Clara, Dreaming: A Futuristic Romance Retelling of The Sandman Retelling (Foxwept Array #2)

Lissa, Beautiful: A Futuristic Romance Retelling of The Frog Princess (Fowept Array #4)

THE ARTILECT WAR

The Seeds of Winter: Artilect War Book One

The Gardener of Man: Artilect War Book Two

The Harvest of Souls: Artilect War Book Three

The Artilect War Complete Series

Printed in the USA
CPSIA information can be obtained
at www.ICGtesting.com
LVHW041449230624
783806LV00028B/235

9 781999 571177